W9-BXF-835

Depth of Field

Sue Hubbard

Acknowledgements

Thanks are due to Martin Crucefix, Simon Morley,
Mario Petrucci and Wendy Rawlings for their insightful
comments on the work in progress; to Marianne Lewin for
her hospitality whilst working on the manuscript and to
Alan Tomlinson for endless photocopying and proofreading.
I am also indebted to the Corporation of Yaddo,
Saratoga Springs, for its generous support
whilst revising the final version.

First published in the United Kingdom in April 2000 by

Dewi Lewis Publishing
8 Broomfield Road, Heaton Moor
Stockport SK4 4ND, England
+44 (0)161 442 9450

All rights reserved

The right of Sue Hubbard to be identified as author of this work
has been asserted by her in accordance with the
Copyright, Designs and Patents Act 1988.

Copyright ©2000
For the text: Sue Hubbard
For this edition: Dewi Lewis Publishing
Front cover photograph: Helen Sear

ISBN: 1-899-235-82-5

Printed and bound in Great Britain by
Biddles Ltd, Guildford and King's Lynn

3 5 7 9 8 6 4 2

First Edition

Depth of Field

Sue Hubbard

DEWI LEWIS
PUBLISHING

As a living soul, I am the very contrary of history,
I am what belies it, destroys it for the sake of my own history.
Roland Barthes

The camera is my tool.
Through it I give reason to everything around me.
André Kertész

Setting the focus

I am in the dark. This small room is like a nun's cell. Everything in its place. Neat, spare and entirely functional. There is a sink, the developing trays, a shelf of chemicals. Above the workbench the safety lamp glows a womb-like red. I have got used to doing things by feel or touch, by intuition. On the other wall, away from the water is an enlarger and a stack of boxes containing different grades of photographic paper and my books. The walls are bare except for a small spot where the paint peeled when I finally took down the photo of Liam. It left a small patch like pale new skin after a sticking plaster has been removed. In the developing trays black and white shapes are beginning to emerge from the bromide like thin ghosts. They seem to come out of nowhere, fragile as those transparent moths that gathered in our garden porch, clustering round the storm lantern on late summer evenings. They surface silent as memories and like the moths will only last for a while until they too perish; their paper yellowing or torn, lost or crumpled at the back of some dark damp drawer. Born from silver grains, they will eventually begin to age, will suffer attacks of light, of humidity; fade, weaken, and then vanish. Once transcendence was achieved through remembrance; through the images we keep in our head, or a smell, a taste, the chance sound of a voice. Perhaps it isn't coincidence that this is the century that invented both photography and history. But whereas history is simply a construct, the photograph is a device through which we try, for a brief moment, to hold time still before it moves relentlessly, indifferently on.

Sometimes I work listening to music. To Bach's late cello concertos or a Brahms *intermezzo*. But this morning I need quiet. Being here in this silence, among the faint whiff of chemicals reminds me of the labour room, of all that whiteness. Only the dull electronic blip, that thin line pulsating on the green screen monitoring the foetal heart beat, the sound of my own breathing; the icy tiles and starched linen.

Through my lens I have raised them from murky obscurity. Particularised and named them. In a way given them birth. Mary, Winston, the small girls with black braids like oiled rope, in pink nylon dresses, skipping. The abandoned synagogue in Princelet Street.

In order to obtain a positive picture, in which the light and shade corresponds to the original subject, it is necessary to print the negative. Everything contains the potential to be its opposite.

Exposure

Snapshot: A stone cottage on the side of a hill just before it descends into the elbow of a valley. Smoke from the chimney-stack speckles the lilac tree with black smuts. Frozen nappies flap stiffly on the line, a row of white bunting.

Belongings cover the kitchen table, overflow onto the flag floor from tea chests and apple boxes. Books on photography and gardening, a Blue Peter Annual, a single small wellington boot. Sets of saucepans, jam jars, a measuring jug. Rusty baking tins.

It took so long to construct. The patchwork cushions, the lemon balm and pots of geraniums wintering on the window sill. I didn't know what was expected, so gathered the russet windfalls with their musty yellow skins and chopped and chopped and boiled and stewed until the kitchen was filled with the fumes of pickling vinegar, as if our lives depended on it.

The furniture is packed away. The goat's already gone to the neighbours. The chickens have been slaughtered. No one would take them. They were too old and their egg production not up to much. I was simply being sentimental not wanting to kill them. That shows I never became a real country person, despite the baking, the yoghurt and wine making. None of the farm workers in the village would have kept chickens that didn't lay. They'd have wrung their necks.

Now the city beckons. Its street markets brimming with sweet potatoes, mangoes, rubbish and noise. I came to the country to try and set down roots in the loamy Somerset soil. Now we are to return to grey streets and row upon row of anonymous red brick Victorian villas where we know no one. Where I and the children will simply merge with all the other beige washed-out faces.

✳

The day we leave the valley it snows. The first cold snap. The sky lies in a grey blanket over the ploughed fields. The cabbages are frilled with rime. The summer runners have turned yellow, the un-picked pods shrivelled as old men's fingers in the frost. Leaves from the copper beech crunch like broken glass underfoot. "Hurry up Mum, its freezing. Josh is taking up *all* the room. M-u-m he won't move." The children sit wrapped in scarves and anoraks, shivering in the car with the tabby cat mewing and scratching on their laps, terrified in its wicker basket, while I dig at the iron ground. Christmas roses. I planted them when we moved into the cottage. They are the only thing in bloom in the bare January garden, hidden behind the black-boughed lilac tree by the hen coop. Now the hens have gone, the woodshed is empty. We are leaving. And all the while I try to blot out Tom's insistent voice: *Hannah. I'm telling you, if you persist, I'll hold you responsible if...*

I wrap the frail white blooms in black plastic bin liners and old newspaper, my fingers clumsy in the sharp morning air. I want to take them with me, those bruised white flowers. One last living connection. I hope they will live in my London garden.

✳

A dog barks, a lorry changes gear in the street below as I huddle back under the duvet, into the hollow indentation of the mattress, enjoying the frowsty warmth. The sheets feel coarse against my bare skin. They're grubby. I should change them but I like the familiar body smell. A childhood smell. When I was little I used to dribble on the pillow like an animal marking its territory. A cistern gurgles and splutters through ancient pipes in another part of the building. Coffee mugs, drawings, photographs litter the floor. Dirty tights lie on the chair like shed skins. Through the rattan blinds the early morning seeps like stale sleep. I like this room. My room. With its pale apricot walls, its wooden floor. There is hardly any furniture. Just a low futon, a chair and my Turkish rugs, a couple of posters, some drawings and a few photographs. I've arranged it to suit myself. I can be selfish now. Books line the shelves by the stove, along with the pots of lemon balm brought from Somerset. And beside them are pictures of the children as chubby babies, naked and sunburnt, chasing the hens across the grass. If I close my eyes for a moment I can hear their small high voices floating across the lawn:

– *Shoo Sally Henny Penny you big fat thing. Back to your pen, back to your pen. Annie quick, quick...*

I find it hard to distinguish between the two. To tell from the photographs which is Josh and which is Annie. Both have the same round cherubic faces and pudding-basin haircuts, both wear the same hand-me-down dungarees and striped T-shirts. And for a moment I am filled with sadness and a sense of loss and grief that we cannot go back and do it all again, that it cannot be mended. I think of Annie sitting in a nappy on the path by the lavender bush on a hot summer afternoon, holding the striped spiral of a snail-shell in her fat muddy hand, her cheeks streaked with earth. She is peering into the dark visceral orifice to see where it's gone. Slowly it pokes out its head. She talks to it, cajoling and encouraging it out to eat a leaf, stroking its rubbery grey horns with a fat finger. Or Josh down by the hawthorn making a dam of stones and brushwood to change the course of the stream.

On the wall, above the wicker chair, is a large poster of Pissaro's *Girl with a Switch*. It connects me back to the valley, to what I know we've lost. To the idyll I naively believed for so long was possible. The long blue shadows of the late summer afternoon, the young girl's indolence as she trails her switch through the grass, the loll of her head under the big sun bonnet in the heavy heat, all remind me of the particular peace that I thought, just for a moment, we had found.

✳

For a long time after he left I still wore my wedding ring. As if by wearing it I could defy what had happened. Then the day we left for London, as Josh and Annie sat waiting in the packed car, the cat scratching in her basket on their laps, I pulled it off and buried it in the garden under the lilac tree. My finger was white, indented where it had cut into flesh all those years. I thought of my Great-grandmother, here in the East End, the East End to which we have returned. Her raw hands. Swollen from hot water and harsh soap. The tight band cutting into chipolata fingers. I kept searching for it with my thumb as if I'd accidentally lost something. The mark stayed for months. I watched it fade as my finger began to plump out, take on its old shape like someone ill putting back weight after a long convalescence.

London is freezing. The sky an endless canopy of unremitting grey. I'm worried every time the kids go out, convinced they will be abducted and never come back.

"Josh if you are going to play with a friend you must tell me

10

where you're going. Do you understand?"

"Mum, I'm nearly twelve, don't fuss."

I wait outside the wire netting of the playground for Annie to come out of school clutching a wodge of letters about nits and teacher in-training days. I dread the post. Tom's letters:

Hannah,

If you are having problems with Josh, you have no one to blame but yourself. Your selfishness at dragging the children to live in the East End of London, simply for your own ends, some bizarre scheme, illustrates just how little you put their needs before your own. If they had come here, Alison and I could have offered them the sort of stability that you will never be able to manage. But it is of little surprise to me that you put your desires before their best interests.

Tom

My parents come to visit. Their faces are drawn tight with disapproval at finding Josh skate boarding with the boys from the flats on the estate opposite.

"Hey man that's wicked. How d'you do that?"

"There are two *T*s in the middle of 'better' Joshua," my father says, as we sit down to vegetable lasagne at the table I've carefully laid among the still unpacked tea chests.

Slowly we begin to settle into our life. The children go to school and I to work part-time in the bookshop. I miss Marion and her northern good sense, am sustained by phone calls. Without her friendship I'd never have survived Tom's leaving let alone the move. I scour the markets for cheap food and possible material for photographs. Ridley Road market. The stalls piled high with yams, sweet potatoes and purple aubergines shiny as the maybugs that fell through my bedroom window in Somerset. Green and yellow okra, outsized ladies knickers, cheap cutlery and saucepans.

"25p a quarter top quality mush. How you doing then Josh, me son?"

Sunday mornings we drive across to the Heath. In the land-scaped grounds of Kenwood couples walk arm in arm in waxed barbours and thick scarves, carrying fat sheaves of Sunday papers or balancing toddlers on unstable tricycles. High above the Vale of Health anoraked fathers uncoil flapping kites into the north London wind, as Josh and Annie look embarrassed at my efforts to launch their flat plastic dragon which keeps crash landing at my feet.

"Really it doesn't matter Mum."

I try to find hooks to connect us as we float, rootless as green algae on the surface of a stagnant pond, to this new life. And all the while my camera lies unused, on the dresser, waiting for me to get out and explore the streets.

✳

This is the first day of my new regime, of going out after I've dropped the kids at school to take pictures. The sun has gone in again. Sometimes I can't quite believe that this is where I have ended up. That I left that narrow Somerset lane with its high stone walls, smelling in spring of wood sorrel and wild garlic, to come here.

Mile End Road. A grey cambric sky. The wind snips and snaps like a pair of tailor's scissors. Birth place of the Sally Army and home to Christopher Wren's Trinity Almshouses constructed for '28 *decayed masters and commanders of ships or widows of such'*. A ray of sun peers through the low cloud onto the yellow brick and gleaming plate-glass of the new Bass Charrington brewery. The front has been landscaped. A green oasis in the drab, fume-filled surrounds, sandwiched between the garage offering reconditioned tyres, re-sprays and MOTs, and a boarded-up cinema. Every so often, among the Halal butchers, the laundrettes, and the betting shops, a perfect Georgian façade has survived to be reclaimed in a welter of scaffolding. Litter swirls across the pavement. Crisp packets, sheets of muddy pink newspaper from an old *Loot* flap past the curry house, the junk shop and Arthur Luck & Son Funeral Parlour. The great store of Wickhams and Gardiners, once a respectable East London landmark has gone. Instead there is the Direct Bargain Centre and a Blockbuster Videos. Now Mile End is the feed road to the M11, the eastern escape route from London to Cambridge, Newmarket and the Fens, where the traffic forms a constant arterial clot.

I lift my camera and adjust the aperture. A notice on the rusted gate announces: *Swan Fashions. Wholesalers of Leather, Suede and Sheepskin.* A broken hoarding advertises for: *Machinist, special machinist, cutter, living in machinist, top presser, Hoffman presser.*

I shiver. There is a chill in the air. It's impossible to make out whether or not these are current vacancies. Huguenots, Jews, Bengalis. Generations of pins, scissors and thread. A palimpsest of sweated labour, dreams and despair. The single leaking tap in a filthy tenement. The hours of grinding work in dank ill-lit workshops. A new language heavy on the tongue as a mouthful of pebbles. I go for a medium exposure, reducing the F-stop by one in the hope that I'll be able to catch the ageing layers of peeling paint. This is where I will begin.

✳

I come upon it quite by chance, hurrying back for breakfast before it rains. The inscription is set in a wall and engraved on stone, a sort of matt slate, in tasteful looping script: *On this site stood a house occupied for some years by Captain James Cook. F.N. F.R. 1728-1779. Circumnavigator and Explorer.*

The son of an agricultural labourer from Marton Cleveland, what could have drawn Cook to the sea? Deep furrows etched by cart horses, fetlocks heavy with loam, were the only waves he could have known as a child. Apprenticed at twelve to a haberdasher in Staithes near Whitby, his days consisted of sweeping the floor and polishing mahogany cabinets, of learning to measure yards of ribbon for the Mayor's daughter, of lifting bales of fustian and lengths of camisole lace back and forth from the high shelves. What did he dream of at night? The smell of salt? The sirens' call? The shrill cry of winged griffins or apes which spoke like men? What led him from stays to straits, from whalebone corsets to whalesong? How did a haberdasher's assistant metamorphose from hose and lace to chronometers and calculus?

Late at night he must have sat in his cabin reading Copernicus demolishing Ptolemy's hypothesis of celestial spheres, the waves pounding the bow of his ship, his eyes scratchy with tiredness, as they headed full of hope into the Atlantic. Or sat on the deck, one iris close against the lens of a telescope, charting the moon move across a cloudless sky in an elliptical orbit around the earth, while the earth and planets followed harmoniously in their own paths around the sun.

Then on 13th July 1772, he set sail for the Antarctic without once discovering land. He must have thought he'd reached the mouth of hell as the sky shot through with luminous electrical streamers of pink and blue and gold. The Aurora Australis. Antipodean goddess of light. He covered more than 20,000 leagues, nearly three times the equatorial circumference of the earth, before turning from those lands of ice and heading back to the sun where he met his death in a skirmish on a beach in Hawaii. Back home he was modestly rewarded by King George and made a posthumous baronet and a pension was settled on his widow. Perhaps she grew old alone, on her endowment, in her widow's black poke bonnet, here in this very place.

Standing among these grimy remnants of 18th century London, the traffic flowing past on its way to the Isle of Dogs, I wonder whether, hanging in his hammock late a night, the rain pounding against the deck, the wind in the mainsail, he dreamt of hearth and home, of a warm nuptial bed in Mile End, of his days as a boy, pockets filled with stones to scare the crows. What obsessions, what private daemons drove him? What chimeras or ghosts? What made a farm lad sail more than three times round the world?

✳

I get back to the flat just before the heavens open and as I'm hanging up my jacket hear a sudden violent shouting on the landing below. It sounds like the girl downstairs. She lives with a man I've never seen. I hardly know her. She's just a nod on the communal stairs. I hear her coming in and going out. Her day ends as mine begins. That's the difference in London. I don't know my neighbours. A door slams in the flat below.

"I'll fucking kill you, I'll swing for you you bitch."

The shouting downstairs is followed by a muffled cry and several bangs. I stick my head out of the front door and hear a shuffling followed by strangled sobs and more swearing. Then another door slams and a car in the street revs angrily and drives off. In the stairwell I find the girl who lives below me lying in a crumpled heap on the floor. Her white silk blouse is covered with blood.

"Fucking, bloody bastard. Thinks he owns me the fucking cunt."

"Are you all right?" I ask feebly from the landing above her crumpled shape, immediately regretting the stupidity of my question.

"What the fuck does it look like?"

I go down and gingerly help her up, not knowing whether she'll welcome this. Her lip is swollen and bloody. A red weal is beginning to spread across her right cheek. Her silk blouse has been ripped at the shoulder. I guide her back upstairs and into my flat, feeling the weight of her body sag limply against my hip. She staggers a little, soft flesh against mine, like a bundle of tumble-dried clothes, fresh from the launderette, still holding its warmth. Her skin gives off a sweet smell like stale vanilla. Although she's ten, fifteen years younger than me, her body is beginning to pad out, the tight lycra of her mini-skirt is pulled slightly into a fan of creases, spreading in a V from the point between her thighs. I steady her down onto the futon and go in search of cotton wool and witch hazel.

"What happened? Would you like me to take you down to Casualty?"

"No. I'm OK. Just looks a bloody mess…Won't be the first time, fucking bastard…One day I'll grill his balls. Do something nasty to him in his sleep."

Her voice is taut as cat gut, her still shaking hand belying the apparent bravura of her words as she brushes a strand of bleached hair out of her swollen eye.

"Any chance of a fag or a cup of tea?"

Despite the apparent brio, there's something inappropriately trusting and childlike about her. The heavy kohl and mascara is smudged in sooty runs through her thick foundation like tracks left by rain on a dirty window.

"Who was he?" I inquire cautiously from the kitchen, ferreting in the back of the cupboard for a tea bag; "not that it's any of my business."

"Oh that's Dave. He's my boss and sometimes my bloke. He can't handle it if he thinks I've been chatting up the punters. He's just a dick-head." And though it must hurt her face to do so, she breaks out into a raucous laugh. "Bloody men. Either want you to fuck them or be their bleeding mothers and half the time they can't bloody decide which. These yours?" she says nodding at the photos of Josh and Annie on the shelf by the lemon balm.

"Yes… Sugar?"

"Two, ta. What sort of tea d'you call this?" she asks grimacing

16

and reaching over to help herself to my tobacco and papers. "This all you got? Sorry don't mind me, I'm just a pushy bitch."

"Sorry, I've only got Earl Grey. I'm not much of a tea drinker. Look, are you sure about the hospital? That eye looks nasty. I know it's nothing to do with me, but perhaps you should tell the police?"

"Na. It's fine. Best thing I can do is go and sleep it off. Thanks for the tea," she says draining the dregs and slowly drawing in the pain, gathering her body back together as if to go. And in her movements I sense there is a certain possessiveness, a strange reluctance to relinquish what has just happened. It is as if she has already washed, dried and ironed the incident – just as she will her damaged shirt – and slipped it away in the back of a drawer like a precious memento ready to be brought out again, good as new, whenever she needs it next.

"Thanks for coming to the rescue. Many round here wouldn't want to know. Shit, look at this blouse. Brand new on. Name's Della by the way."

"Mine's Hannah."

"Nice to meet you, at last, Hannah," she says, rather formally holding out a limp, manicured hand. "Seen you on the stairs when I've been coming in of a morning. Good to know I've a friendly neighbour. Hope you're a better judge of blokes than me," she adds, smiling weakly, as she edges herself cautiously off the futon. And as I hear Tom hectoring about my irresponsibility towards the children, and wonder again, if he's right, that I should never have brought them to London, should have loved them enough to surrender them to his care, to Alison's insistence on music practice, tidy bedrooms and French verbs, more effective, undoubtedly, than mine, I rather doubt it.

"And what do you do then Hannah, if you don't mind me asking?" she says slipping back painfully against the cushions, giving up the attempt to get up and go.

17

"I'm a photographer."

"Classy!" In the circumstances I'm amazed at her good humour. "What you do? Fashion? Travel? Adverts? I expect you get to go to loads of flash places."

"No, nothing so exciting I'm afraid. The furthest I've been for weeks is the Mile End Road. I'm taking photos of the East End. For a gallery. I've been offered my first exhibition. I won a photographic competition and that was the prize. Look can I get you something a bit stronger than tea? You're still very pale. I've some whisky somewhere. A friend left it. I'll never drink it."

"Well I wouldn't say no if you twist my arm. Still feeling a bit shaky," she says taking off her shoes and curling her black stockinged legs beneath her as if settling down to stay. "You haven't been here that long have you, Hannah?"

"Nearly a couple of years now. I can't really believe how quickly the time's gone. I moved up from the country."

"Really? Why would you want to come here then? I've always wanted to move out. A nice house in Essex. Some polo ponies, a pool. That'd suit me fine. Fat chance."

"Did you grow up round here?"

"East End born and bred. Went to school round here. My first job was in my Auntie's laundrette; you know that one on the corner. Seen enough of other people's grubby knickers to last me a lifetime. I'm a croupier now. Dave's got a club in Mare Street. Just up past the Hackney Empire. Perhaps you've seen it, the one with the smoky glass in the windows. We get all sorts. Boxers, DJs. Look, you've been really great," she says draining her whisky, "but I think I'll make a move. Try and get a bit of shut eye while Dave's cooling off somewhere," she says, tentatively touching her cheek.

"If you're sure you'll be OK? I'm off to work in a while but you can always give me a shout if you need anything."

"Cheers Hannah. Look, when I've got me face back, come and

have a drink one evening if you fancy. That's if we're ever up the same time. I'm a bit of a night owl. Anyway really appreciate the help. See you later then," she says crossing gingerly to the door as if the slightest small movement causes her pain.

Outside it's started to rain. Coloured umbrellas dot the unbroken grey of the street. Wet tyres on tarmac. A taxi pulls up. I can't see who gets out and wonder if perhaps it's Dave come back to check the damage now he's cooled down and contrite. I can hear the engine ticking over, and then a rev as it pulls off in a flurry of spray leaving a purple film of petrol floating on the puddles.

✳

Some things take hold in the mind as metaphors. History needs to find its equivalence in the personal and the present. Memory is a resurrection of a kind. A photograph does not necessarily tell us about what no longer is, but only and for certain, what has been. We photograph things in order to drive them from our minds, to place them outside ourselves rather than let them live flitting inside our heads like shadowy moths. Painting can aspire to a kind of reality without ever actually having experienced it. But in a photograph the real thing once stood in front of the small black eye of the lens. What was caught is the actual moment when the subject was simply itself: an old man with a cataract, a lily dropping yellow pollen on a white cloth, a church clock stuck at five to three, before it became an eternal subject for another's gaze.

✳

Sunday morning. From the Mosque in Whitechapel High Street, an electronic mullah calls the faithful to prayer. Bearded men in white lace skullcaps drift out from among stalls selling cut-price trainers, cheap transistors, and day-glo T-shirts. From Brick Lane the smell of chicken tikka and vindaloo floats across the street under the frilled net curtains of the curry houses. Cumin and coriander.

The old market at Spitalfields has gone. Moved out to the wastes of Hackney marshes among the high-rises and the link roads. But Brick Lane still teems. Mangoes, sweet potatoes, pyramids of green and yellow tufted corn and okra. Prawns by the pint and pots of gritty winkles in vinegar. The air shudders with the banging of hammers, the grinding of developers' drills. First these streets were filled with refugees, then artists came looking for low rents. Now the swathe of gentrifiers and corporations is moving in to add a little colour, a touch of chic bohemianism. Builders scrub and blast the sandstone facades of the neglected eighteenth century houses, strip the wood back through generations of paint on shutters that once closed out the smog-filled London night from the tiny candle-lit parlours of Huguenot weavers and lace makers.

Quaker Street. Fleur-de-Lis Street. Elder Street. The names echo like a litany. I imagine long pale faces, sombre coarse black cloth, and starched linen. Days of work, of prayer. Measured God-fearing days.

In a grimey window, past the boarded up shop fronts, the boutiques selling discounted leather jackets and tapes of Indian music, mirror-work and incense, the display in Mr. Weinburg's printing shop charts the stream of emigrations and migrations on the note-paper headings. *Minsky (Furs) Whitechapel, Manchester and Bradford; Elegante Fashions, Berwick St; The Nazral – genuine Bengali cooking.* Re-location cards announce that David Glassman – once perhaps Labovitch the Glazier – *will be moving to new premises in Golders Green. Rozansky Fashions* now has a metal grill over the window and a 'to let' sign outside. A new wine merchant's has opened next to C.H. Katz, the shop that has nothing in its windows but huge balls of twine and string. I turn right down Princelet Street, past the restored 18th century houses, their wooden panelling waxed and stripped, the rooms filled with stylish contemporary paintings and Victorian antiques. I am looking for 19, Princelet Street, for the old synagogue that is now a Jewish Heritage Centre. There is only a discreet brass nameplate screwed to the heavy wooden door. The façade is unrestored, crumbling. Inside the ochre walls are stippled and foxed with damp, the empty arc filled with jam jars of dead flowers. The brass chandelier and wooden fretwork decorating the upper balcony make it look more like a Quaker meeting house than a synagogue squeezed into the garden plot at the back of this old Huguenot house.

The plaster is stained and faded. The high windows only let in a little indirect light. In the women's balcony the dusty wooden benches still seem to be waiting for their former occupants; for Leah Schonfeld and Dolly Rosenthal in her new felt hat. I try to imagine the cantor's voice counterpointed against a patter of November rain, the candles flickering across the Hebraic names gilded on the brown wood panelling. This is why I came. To try and recapture something of what it must have been like for my grandfather, arriving here from Harwich via the Hook of Holland with his family, carrying everything they owned in a few bundles. The samovar, the silver candlesticks, the parchment exit papers stamped by the Czar. Frightened, lost, speaking nothing but Yiddish. Wandering Jews dropped, by chance or accident on the Isle of Dogs, because in the scramble on a crowded quay, among the rigging and tall masts, the mewing gulls, the barking stevedores and smell of herring, they had climbed onto the wrong boat, or because there hadn't been enough money to make it all the way to New York. This has nothing to do with that other London. The leafy roads of Highbury or Primrose Hill, the neat painted Victorian villas of Wandsworth and Fulham, with their ruched curtains and stripped pine front doors, an ageing Volvo full of dog hairs and children's car seats on the kerb outside. This is another country. Foreign. Exotic as Calcutta or the teaming souks of Marrakech.

I know so little. So have to invent the past. I can see the women wrapped in their best fur-collared coats, chenille dresses, hats and wigs covering their shorn hair. My grandmother, perhaps, or my great-aunt? Separate and apart from the body of the service, whispering and gossiping under their breath, as the men get on with the business of worship.

In memory of Mrs. Sarah Deborah Solomons died 31st March 1942. Donated by her children £5. 5s.0d. In memory of H. Rinkoff who died 21st March 1949. Donated by his wife and children £6. 6s. 0d.

But that's wrong. It doesn't fit. The inscriptions are later than the time I'm trying to imagine. It's those who came earlier that concern me. Those, now nameless and unrecorded, flushed out by the pogroms from the Pale of Settlement. By mobs who looted Jewish homes and stores, smashed furniture, their mouths distorted with hate and a dark anger they couldn't even name. I imagine my grandfather, a small white-faced boy, nervously clasping the hand of his father, a man of about forty with a dark beard, as he guards a battered cardboard suitcase on the deck of a crowded steamship. Everywhere there are sickly infants, pale pregnant women, and suspicious young men with ringlets and dusty black coats. From Besarabia, from Vilna, from Kiev and Minsk. Those who set sail from Yalta, from Odessa and Sebastopol expecting who knows what? Those who chose exile rather than conversion or death. Young men barred from making a living in factories or the professions. The *Luftmentshn* who lived by their wits – the people of the air. So bleached and transparent, they lived their lives like undeveloped negatives, afraid of the light.

Now every other shop in Brick Lane is a sari emporium filled with rolls of silver filigree fabric, purple and pink voile embroidered with gold thread. This is an outpost of the Indian sub-continent rather than of Lodz or Warsaw. Even the twenty-four-hour bagel shop has a poster in the window advertising Gudjarati dancers. Most of the Jews I came looking for have gone to their green gardens and tennis courts of Stanmore and Edgware. But just past a new building bearing a sign that announces itself as the Bangladeshi Welfare Association, in the darkened interior of a tiny shop filled with bundles of rags, among the bolts of grimy cloth, the piled off-cuts of nylon fur, an old man, dressed like a rabbi, with full grizzled beard and black homburg, sits at a battered desk holding an improbable conversation on a mobile phone.

In the dark doorway of the Jamme Marjid mosque on the corner of Fournier Street, once a Huguenot church, then a synagogue, men in tunics and white crochet skull caps move silently to and fro among the ghosts of dour French clock-makers in dark woollen clothes and lace collars. Just inside the threshold is a rack of shoes. A smell of incense wafts into the street. On the outside an architect's sign announces: *conversion works for basement ablutions.* It must have been around here that my father grew up. I don't know where exactly. It was not something he has ever talked about. His past was a far off country from which he had escaped when young and never spoke of. Two young Asians, in sharply cut trousers and leather jackets, sit on the steps chatting. Each wears a heavy gold chain inside his open neck shirt. Two little girls in nylon dresses and white socks play skipping: *Ro-sy a-pple, le-mon tart, te-ell mee the na-ame of your sweet heart.*

Their jet hair is oiled and braided into long thick plaits. The rhyme belongs to some forgotten English rural past. While they are absorbed in their game I get out my camera.

On the steps of Christ Church, the Hawksmoor church, an old woman in three overcoats sits surrounded by a bundle of plastic carrier bags. She's mumbling to herself as she sorts out rags, taking them from one bag and cramming them back into another for no obvious reason. Beneath the great coats she wears filthy army boots. Her bare legs are scabbed and caked with dirt. I can smell her from ten yards away. I climb the steps and cautiously try to strike up a conversation, ask if she'd like to have her photograph taken, but she spits at me, showering me with a spray of sputum and tells me, in a thick Irish brogue, to frig off. A pearl of spittle curls down the front of my leather jacket. I mutter an apology and move away quickly. I didn't mean to offend her. I need to be more careful. I don't want to become a voyeur appropriating the small melodramas of other people's lives.

I finish up the last couple of frames on the tombstones in the churchyard – *Not lost but gone before. Asleep in the arms of Jesus 1842* – and walk back up to Brick Lane, past a young man on the junction of Fournier Street selling copies of the Socialist Workers' newspaper, and think how this part of London has always been a potential political fault line. I stop at the Indian sweet shop. It smells wonderful. A mixture of cinnamon and condensed milk. Trays of exotic green confections sit next to squares of treacly pastry covered in pistachio nuts. Jewel-pink jelly mounds float in syrup. I don't know the name of anything. It's like being abroad.

Back in the kitchen I collapse, grubby and exhausted, into the armchair and tip out three rolls of film from my camera-bag onto the kitchen table. Shots of the heritage centre and the market. God knows if any of them'll be any good, if I'll have found what I came looking for. I'm not really hungry and leave the chopped herring bagel in its paper bag, put on the kettle and light a cigarette. Smoke mingles with the steam, as beads of spring rain chase each other down the windowpane.

It seems strange sitting here, at the same kitchen table where Annie and I used to bake bread. It's what she loved to do at the cottage when she came home from play-school. Stand on a chair wrapped in a big T-towel up to her armpits, sleeves pulled around her podgy elbows making concrete jam tarts. She'd spend all afternoon kneading the dirty grey pastry; her upper lip covered in a fine brown moustache of flour, her arms caked with dough, while I pounded the mixture on the deal table. Cutting and slapping it into shape before leaving it to prove on the warm Aga. When Tom came home from the college she'd present them to him laid out on a blue china plate, hard as limestone. She would stand in front of the stove, her arms crossed, watching carefully as he tried not to break his teeth, to make sure he'd finished every crumb.

The surface of the table is pitted with knife marks, etched with heat rings. I used to bleach and scrub it with a bristle brush. Now I don't bother. But I haven't completely abandoned the need to make or grow things. All last summer, on my small balcony, yellow and orange nasturtiums, bought in Columbia Road flower market early one Sunday, spilled like raw pigment from a white ceramic sink. When the weather improves I'll plant some more.

I'm telling you Hannah, if you persist, I promise, I'll hold you responsible...

Lying in the long grass below the cottage after blackberrying with the children, watching the late evening sun sink in a fiery ball behind the hill, I thought I'd come close to finding perfection. That at last I'd found a place I could belong. Happiness, I believed, was an act of will. I could simply make it happen by baking more bread, by arranging moon daisies and wild borage from the high field in a terracotta vase in the window sill. Failure could be held at bay, like Canute holding back the tide, by endless activity, by never looking at the shadows of the past that led us to this place like migratory birds following some inner magnetic pull.

Now there's so much to do. In the morning, when I clean my teeth, my hair pulled back from my face in a rubber band, I can see what I'll look like in fifteen, twenty years. Like my father. The same flesh around the jowls, the same tracery of lines. Memory is etched in the landscape of the body. Outside the window a thrush is busy hammering a snail on the cobbled paving in the yard. I mustn't complain. I have survived in a fashion. Though the Christmas roses died. But they did not choose to come here. They had no need.

✳

The teapot is full of stale leaves. I'm rather enjoying becoming a slut after all those house-proud years. The kettle boils and the smell of fresh coffee fills the kitchen. Outside a thin wisp of sun dances on the red brick wall. Last summer's geraniums stand withered in their window boxes caught by the winter frost. I forgot to bring them in. I wouldn't have done that in the country. Everything there happened according to its right season. Planting, pricking out, bottling and pickling. The fox-stink of the first cream elder flowers, broad as dinner plates, soaked with lemon and sugar in a plastic bucket to make sparkling wine. Dark berries hanging in an old gauze nappy on the iron hook in the pantry, the purple juice dripping into the white enamel basin like blood from the throat of a gamekeeper's hare. But that was another life. I pour some coffee, savouring its bitter tang, the warmth of the mug in my hands, then close my eyes and try to fix the memories like photographs in developing solution. But they dissolve, break up, then slip away.

I don't have to go to the bookshop this afternoon. Today there's something else I need to do. I go back into my bedroom and sitting cross-legged on the Turkish rug, propped against the cushions from the futon, open the green calf album. The black cardboard pages, interleaved with thin sheets of tissue and held together by a frayed gold cord, have faded. I turn them, feeling their thickness, their weight against my legs. There is the other cottage I have been trying to remember, blotted out by the image of the one I left recently. On the first page is a yellowing black and white snapshot. Dots of mildew speckle the surface. It shows a cottage nestling beside a small church. It's not really old, despite its pseudo-Tudor beams, its white brickwork and steep pitched roof. A dentist's surgery, a solicitor's office now perhaps? Swallowed up by suburbia. The pretence of being in the country finally conceding defeat. There is a young man. Stylish, dapper, though his slicked-back hair is growing thin. Four brass RAF buttons decorate the front of his blazer. Between his teeth he clasps the stem of a pipe. I think of all those grainy post-war films, those cravated matinée idols with their strangulated vowels. Yet there's something constricted, tense about the apparently easy smile. On his shoulder he balances, with one hand, like an organ grinder's monkey, a small child in smocked gingham. Wiry copper curls straggle over her dark eyes. She stares ahead, squinting slightly into the sun, serious and unsmiling. I try to remember, but I can't.

And there, in another picture, is my mother in a short floral rayon dress, with square padded shoulders and five clear plastic heart-shaped buttons down the front, her eyes turned coyly from the camera. In her white ankle socks and flat summer sandals she looks like a schoolgirl. It's disconcerting to realise how much older I am now than she was then. She crouches, on the pocket handkerchief lawn, her hands outstretched, as I stagger forward across the green taking my first tentative steps, a large bow attached to a corkscrew curl.

So there we all are. Flat, one dimensional, like characters' names on a script, waiting for a playwright to flesh us into life, to play out our drama. Like clothes left too long in a hot wash, the memories are shrunk, faded and run, all merged into the same shade of dull grey. Only occasionally, like a red cardigan or a blue scarf that escaped being thrown in with the general load, do they hold their colour. But because I can't remember, because it is simply a blank, maybe I can construct it differently. Create myself in my own chosen image. How do I know what really happened anyway? The truth behind these frozen images – what is invention, fiction or fact? History can be re-written however we choose. So I try to reconstruct my own past. I have no guide or compass, no idea where this journey will lead. Time is an unreliable map.

There on the first, dog-eared page is a small boy with dark curly hair, slightly blurred and out of focus. The photograph's attached to the cardboard by transparent paper corners, yellowed and brittle as nail-parings. His worsted shorts are held up by a pair of braces over a hand-knitted tank-top. White legs poke from thick knee-socks concertinaed around his ankles. His face is pinched in concentr-ation as he stands on the steep beach skimming flat stones across the crested waves. I carefully detach it from the page. The gum has turned flaky with age. On the back, written in violet ink, in faded copperplate, it says *Southend-on-Sea 1926*.

The year of the General Strike. Jack Abrahams, my father, aged 10. It's hard to believe he was alive then, at a time my mind has designated as history. My parents' early years are like a well kept secret. It's as if neither of them existed before I was born. I was shocked recently when I read that our great-grandchildren will probably not even know our names.

I imagine him getting ready for the outing. Two copper pennies, a ball of string and a licorice gob stopper nestling in the fluffy lining of his pocket. His Auntie Leah had organised it. 'We'll all go. Blow the old cobwebs away.' It had been a struggle getting the transport. A friend had lent them an old Ford for the day. With the strike Jack's teachers had been arriving at school any way they could, in patched-up old cars, on decrepit bicycles.

So there they all are, stumbling down to the beach, carrying rugs and overcoats, despite the sticky afternoon heat, their dark eyes and sharp profiles out of place among the weather-beaten complexions of the locals, lobster from a week of sun. Fumbling in her leatherette handbag Leah searches for change for a striped deck chair for each of the adults, which they set up, rather self-consciously, high on the sand by the sea wall, well back from the crowds and the incoming tide. Millie unpacks their lunch. Cold roast chicken, matzos, pickled gerkins, a seed cake, carefully wrapped in greaseproof paper inside brown paper bags tied with string.

Jack wanders off across the sands. His thick boots sinking into the soft powdery surface. He can feel them talking about him, see them out of the corner of his eye. There on the far end of the breaker, just off to the left, the local lads in their cable-knit jerseys and scruffy plimsolls, fishing and sharing an illicit packet of Senior Service. They come every day. With their fishing rods and tin cans full of squirming maggots which they buy by the pint from the pet shop. He sees them creep up behind an old man fishing from the promenade and drop a grey maggot into his thermos of tea while he's busy reeling in his line. Jack can feel their eyes running over his inappropriate city clothes, his pallid London skin. One of them has propped his bike up against the sea wall. A shiny black Raleigh bike with a pump and bell. A slither of silver fish flounders in the net slung over the handle bars. Across the grey beach a group of donkeys huddles by the whelk stand. Small girls giggle and tuck their sprigged cotton frocks into their woollen knickers as the donkey-man leads them bobbing across the corrugated sands. Leaving his Ma and Pa and Auntie in their deck chairs, he wanders to the candy floss booth and furtively hands over his 1/2d. "No spending your money on food now Jack. You never know who's touched it, where their hands have been," his Ma had warned. Perched on a breaker he stops to watch the Punch and Judy and two small girls, in frilled sun-bonnets and polka-dot dresses, playing crazy golf with their father. He'd like to live here.

He hated Whitechapel. The narrow tenemented streets, the November fog like dirty lint in the alleys. If he lived here he wouldn't have to go to Bar Mitzvah classes, or put up with Rabbi Rabinovitz, with his piggy eyes and bad breath, rapping him across the knuckles with a wooden ruler when he stumbled through the *Talmud*. It was stupid learning Hebrew, only Jews learnt Hebrew. What was the point of learning a dead language hardly anyone spoke? He wasn't even sure there was a God anyway. Recently he'd started to argue about the Sabbath visits to the Machzikei Hadath. But his Ma would hurry him out of the front door, dabbing his mouth with a knob of spit on the corner of her white handkerchief, his hair slicked with water, *yarmulke* pinned to the back of his head, boots polished.

✳

Sitting on the sand, enjoying the sugary threads of candy-floss dissolve against the roof of his mouth he dreams of having a black Raleigh bike he can ride without holding onto the handles. He's fed up. Nothing ever happens. Every Friday night there's the same old ritual. Chopped liver, sweet red wine, candles and prayers. Then Sunday afternoons tea at Auntie Leah's and the stultifying chatter, over a game of canasta, about Mr. Weinberg's prostate operation or how it's time Becky Greenstein settled down and what a pity it is she doesn't do something about that moustache. When he'd been smaller it hadn't been so bad. He'd taken his Meccano set, and while the adults talked, had constructed bridges and pulleys behind the arm of the sofa. He wanted to be an engineer when he grew up and build bridges and skyscrapers. He saved every 1/2d until he could afford a new wheel or a shiny red sprocket. The minute he'd had enough he'd be off to Wolf's toy shop at the end of Middlesex Street. All his money was spent on extravagant and rare parts which he kept in an old cigar box lined with dark blue silk. He'd found it on a stall in Petticoat Lane. The man had let him have it for 6d as the lid was broken and needed gluing. But he was too old now to sit on the floor making things. He hated having to listen to his Auntie's Caruso and Chaliapin records week after week. She'd slip them out of their paper sleeves, carefully blowing off the imagined dust, then wind up the walnut gramophone and make everybody be quiet, as she sat back in the easy chair with a cup of tea and a piece of caraway cake. He hated the way she reached down the front of her dress between her two big wobbling breasts for her lace hanky to dab her eyes, overcome with the emotion of the music, though she'd heard it a hundred times before.

Perhaps he should run away to sea, he thinks, trickling sand over the toes of his boots. Join the Navy. See the world. Africa, New Zealand, perhaps America. He could go to New York and see the Statue of Liberty. Or maybe he should join the RAF and become an airman.

As he pokes the bare candy floss stick into the sand, the hair on the back of his neck bristles. He doesn't move, sensing the boy with the bike he saw fishing on the breaker, standing beside him. He is about fourteen with a spongy freckled face and sandy hair.

"What you doing Jew-boy, digging to Australia?"

※

In this photo he must be what? Sixteen? Seventeen? It's hard to tell with that short back and sides, the baggy blazer and tie. He is standing outside the school gates, an arm cockily resting across his friend Frank's shoulder. He couldn't wait to leave school after Matriculation. Bright enough his reports said, if only he would apply himself. But he wasn't interested in studying. He would rather hang round kicking a football in the yard than go to the library and study after school. Once he'd gone with some boys to see the *Wembley Wizards*. "Grown mens running around like *meshuga* after a ball," his Ma had moaned. "You miss school for that."

31

When I was small, and my parents were out for the evening, I would creep into the drawing room while Mrs. Watson was ironing the damp sheets she had taken from airing on the pulley over the boiler in the back kitchen, and get out this green calf album from the bottom drawer of the bureau. It seemed so big then. Here is my father in uniform. The leather bomber jacket, the cap and wings, the braid, the familiar pipe at the corner of the mouth, the constructed, slightly uneasy smile. He's with a group of fighter pilots. They're full of the brag of youth, posed along the fuselage of a Spitfire. He can't be more than twenty-one. Most of them, he told me one day, in an uncharacteristic moment of intimacy, never came back, were blown right out of the sky. But no one ever talked about it afterwards. Each buried his grief, his terror that he'd be next, behind a carapace of banter. And all the time, in the mess, he listened. Listened to the timbre of their rounded vowels, to their jokes. Picked up names which he'd memorise like the cipher to a secret code. Jermyn Street, Coutts, The Savile Club. Wearing a uniform allowed him to blur the edges of the past. Humour and charm became his talismens. He began to wear a white silk scarf nonchalantly knotted at the throat of his flying jacket. It was his trade mark. He became the life and soul of the party. His was a good war.

"Come on chaps, let's do a show for the boys. Anyone sing? Who knows a WAF with good legs?"

So he organised the mess show and told a few jokes, and they laughed and slapped him across the shoulders and stood him a pint. He was one of the lads. He was good value and no one bothered to ask "Who are your parents or where did you go to school?"

Rose was seventeen when they met. He was twenty seven. She'd just joined the WRNS. It was early 1945. They were introduced at a party. She was shy, and a little unsure of herself, despite the new chenille frock, the strappy platform shoes she wore to make herself look older. There was about her a quiet refinement he liked. A touch of class. Unlike the other Jewish girls from Edgware or Stanford Hill, with their bright red lips and off the shoulder gowns revealing their full creamy breasts. She was pretty but young. He knew it would be easy to impress her. She hadn't been around much.

She was, she told him one Sunday, when he borrowed a friend's car to take her for the afternoon to Hampton Court, an only child. Her grandfather had been a diamond dealer in Amsterdam.

"Not that I ever knew him," she laughed nervously, running her fingers through her hair to free her dark curls after taking off her hat. They'd walked along the river in the heavy June heat, throwing bread to the ducks. "They had to leave, to get out. It got too dangerous, I suppose".

"My Grandmother believed in education," she continued as they took tea and fairy cakes, served by a waitress in a black satin dress, white starched cap and apron, in the Tea Rooms. "She used to say to her boys 'you'll get a good education if it kills me' and I think it nearly did. She took in washing. I remember her hands. Raw from years of harsh soap. She was a 'sweater'. She sewed button holes by hand for a tailor called Levitch. If each one wasn't perfect it would be sent back and she wouldn't get paid. She picked up the jackets from the factory from the cutters and machinists, then took them all back again for the pressers to finish off with heavy steam irons. She earned 3s 9d. Then she'd cook and scrub for her sons. She kept the money in a pouch pinned to her long knickers under her serge skirt. She bullied her boys. She never let up. Made them study late into the night until they were completely exhausted. The youngest was my father. Oh, I'm so sorry," she laughed nervously patting a stray curl that had escaped from beneath her felt hat "would you like another cup of tea? Shall I pour? Forgive me, I do run on."

Is this right? How can I know half a century later, lying in this quiet book-lined room. The past is like a lump of dough. I have to knead it into recognisable shape. By trying to reconstruct, perhaps it becomes more real than actual events. Maybe that's all that counts in the end. A sense of continuity, an overall meaning.

They went to tea dances, jitterbugged to Glenn Miller and waltzed to a three piece orchestra playing Vera Lynn's *Th-e-re'll be blu-ue bi-rds over the Whi-te cliffs of Do-ver* in hotel ballrooms filled with exotic palms. They ate salmon paste bridge rolls and cucumber sandwiches from silver trays. Once, on the way home, he tried to slip his hand inside her satin blouse but she pulled away.

"It's all right. I can wait. We'll be married soon."

Before the wedding she'd read books, books that you could get from the clinic if you said you were engaged. But still she couldn't quite imagine it, what married people actually did, and was a little afraid. Jack liked her fear. It made him feel safe.

❋

So here is my mother Rose. Dark, softly crimped hair, neat and pretty, sitting by a glowing coal fire skimming her new library book from Boots, the standard lamp with its fringed shade casting long shadows over the wing of her chair. The heavy curtains drawn tight against the damp November dusk. Tea laid on a tray. There's a white lace doily and bone china cups, and Uncle Mac's Children's Hour on the wireless. I'm sitting on the floor cutting out old magazines: *The Picture Post*, *The London Illustrated News*, *John Bull* and pasting them with cow gum into a special commemorative scrapbook with a Union Jack on the front.

"Be careful darling, don't cut over the edge," she says looking up and putting down her book to show me how to use the scissors, how to cut carefully round the edges of the shapes. We're making a memento of the Coronation, but my hands are too clumsy and I'm still too small to care about neatness, as I snip off the dead King's head and paste him next to the two smiling Princesses in their golden coach.

Bending in front of the fire to light his pipe with a coloured spill my father sighs and turns to pour another whisky. A bottle of *Johnnie Walker* always stands beside a small cut-glass jug of water on the round rosewood table, ready for when he comes home at 7.00. First he hangs his overcoat and bowler hat on the stand at the bottom of the mahogany banisters, then he goes straight into the sitting room to pour a drink and read the paper. When I go and kiss him good night, powdered, bathed, ready for bed in my woollen dressing-gown, he smells of whisky and *Balkan Sobranie.*

Meetings, memos, mergers. He must have had another hard day in the City. I knew nothing of his life once he had left with his rolled umbrella and bowler hat for the station, caught the train to the office. He simply vanished, like the white rabbit I'd once seen a conjurer make disappear into a top hat at someone's birthday party. His mellow, modulated tones must have reassured his clients about their overdrafts, investment plans, their shares. But underneath the anxiety was simmering, every five or ten years to erupt in flakes of raw and peeling skin. The anxiety that one day someone might ask casually over a drink while waiting for the 6.15 from Waterloo, "What school's the tie old chap? Were you Oxford or Cambridge?" and he would be found out. An impostor, a fraudster. The Dreyfus in their midst.

On the mantelpiece, the brass carriage-clock ticks into the silence as, back to the fire, feet astride, he unscrews the stem of his pipe and pokes the bowl with a wire pipe cleaner.

"What's for dinner, Rose?" he asks without turning round, emptying the charred ash with two small taps against the fender.

"Fish pie dear," his young wife smiles, looking up eagerly from the cutting out.

"Pity! Had a big lunch at the Club. I'm not really very hungry," and he presses a fresh strand of tobacco from his leather pouch into the cleaned bowl with his right thumb and forefinger, picks up the *Evening Star* and settles himself in the wing chair by the fire. And from my silent cutting out on the floor, I watch the corners of her lips bunch and tighten, her clenched knuckles grow white.

✳

When we first moved to London from the country I thought we'd never survive. That first night, I couldn't believe it never really became dark. A sickly orange glow spread across the city like a halo. The nights at the cottage were so black you couldn't see your hand held out in front of you and in summer shooting stars burst and fizzed across the sky. I felt so guilty, as if I was tearing the children up by the roots. Taking them from the valley where Josh had spent hours building dams, swinging out from the hillside on the rubber tyre he'd fixed to a tree. How could I take them out of a school where they knew the name of every child, and the cows, their pink udders hard and swollen, their swinging backsides steaming, lolloped through the playground at milking time? They'd become real country children, their voices thick with West Country burr. What did they know about cities?

My parents were angry. "Hannah why on earth the East End? Why Bethnal Green of all places? You really ought to think about the children. What about schools? You could live in Putney or Fulham. Somewhere with green spaces, parks, a better type of child. Frankly you're being very irresponsible."

And still I don't know if the pictures will be good enough. If any of it will have been worth it.

✳

Sunday morning. Outside the sky is wide and high and blue.

36

Yesterday there was another affidavit in the post from Tom. He refuses to talk to me, slams down the phone when I ring and says I need to speak to his solicitor if I have anything to say. He seems to have declared war. It's as though through Alison's influence I no longer exist. From the start she has done her best to persuade him that I'm a non-person. She knew that would be the only way he could cope with his guilt about leaving. He can't face seeing himself as a man who could do that to his wife and children. Ever since they met at that wretched conference she's been boring her way into our lives. All those letters she wrote to him under the guise of research, all the time working on him, wearing him down, flattering him that a man of his intelligence couldn't be expected to stay with an hysteric like me. I feel as though I've ceased to exist, to have any feelings. Like two foreign powers they have rallied against me as their common enemy.

The children are becoming argumentative and clingy. Josh vanishes after school without telling me where he is going. I'm terrified as he disappears into the vast city and I ring around his friends. In the country I knew who they were, but here they're just names: Sam, Buzz, Joe. Busy professional mothers, with husbands, are frosty when I phone for the second and third time when he still hasn't come home. "Mum, you're always on my case. No other mothers go on like you. You're the only one," he says banging his bike out of the front door and down the stairs to get away from my excess of anxiety. I don't know where he's going and when I ask he doesn't answer. I hear the bottom door slam. Annie just mooches around. She used to sit for hours in the garden in Somerset drawing, playing in the garden, making up games with stones and flowers. Now she sits in front of the television combing her Barbie's hair. This weekend when they come back they'll be even worse. It seems that everything I say, Tom just contradicts when they are with him. Is it surprising they are confused? Alison is the authority on everything. Apparently she calls me 'that woman' to their faces. The

panic because I couldn't cope with the bored willowy girls standing outside the changing rooms as I struggled to do up impossible zips and fastenings. Humiliated and cross we went and took refuge in the Photographic Museum where I discovered the Daguerreotypes and the small wooden boxes that Fox Talbot had had made by local craftsmen in nearby Lacock. But it was Julia Cameron who obsessed me. A Victorian gentlewoman married to a member of the Indian civil service; she hadn't been given a camera until her 48th birthday. I loved the dreamy romantic portraits she'd taken of Mary, her maid, with her thick Pre-Raphaelite hair, dressed as 'The Angel of the Sepulchre' or the 'Kiss of Peace'. I spent hours looking at the images by unknown local photographers. The two boys standing in baggy shorts on the gate of the level crossing, waiting for the signal to halt the snarling steam train, or the village tea party, with the long trestle table and copper tea urn laid out in the cobbled street lined with bunting. I knew, then, that this was what I wanted to do.

When I examine the string of drying negatives I am pleased with some of the shots of the Heritage Centre in Princelet Street. But I need to go back. This is just the beginning.

This morning by the entrance to the tube at Aldgate East a tramp appeared to be shouting at the sky. He looked quite mad, throwing his arms around in strange stabbing movements. When I drew closer he was singing Verde. *Aida* on a Thursday morning, as the traffic thundered past, for the sheer joy of it.

The two small Bengali girls are beginning to emerge in the developing tray. Their dark braids stand out in stark contrast to their pale nylon dresses. The skipping rope cuts across the frame, an umbilical cord joining them like Siamese twins. There is such poignancy in this frozen moment, this small death. Perhaps that's why I became a photographer, to become an archivist, a cartographer of loss. Above the workbench is the print I made of the James Cook plaque. I imagine him with his compass and sextant, late at night, the wind in the rigging, dividing the sky into constellations. The Pole Star, the Milky Way. Waves of cloudy star streams urging him on.

A grey autumn day. I struggle through. Josh can't find his tie and I'm late getting them to school and they moan that all the others have already gone into class. Leaves scud across the chalked hopscotch squares as I turn and dash for the crowded tube. I am stretched, worn like old elastic, caught between their needs, the imperative to earn money and the desire to get out with my camera. I feel as though I am drowning. At night I wake caught in a spiral of blackness. I dream of swimming in a dark lake. In the cold water green weeds wrap around my limbs and suck me down. It's as if my body no longer exists, is simply a mechanical device to get me through from task to task. Its muscles and sinews yearn for touch. Sometimes I think my heart will simply stop beating for the lack of the feel of another's skin.

✳

It's his voice I notice first. Warm and brown like damp peat. Rain on wet turf. I also notice his hands. Long fingers ending in broad square nails. The raised blue veins close under the surface of the skin. Tactile hands. A writer's, a lover's. But I know I must not think of such things. Desire is too dangerous. I have to learn to make do.

It is such a chance meeting. Synchronicity. But I soon realise that such talk annoys him. He doesn't like what he calls psycho-babble, any more than he likes religion. "So what do you mean Hannah? All those poor bastards shot on the Falls Road? Is that pre-ordained? The pointed finger of G-O-D picking them out? A prior arrangement with a sniper's bullet? Life's more unfair, more random than that. Things are not organised by some omnipotent being just because he thinks we deserve it or it's our turn."

The book he wants is out of stock. So I put in an order. He leaves me his phone number and I say I'll call him when it comes in.

When it arrives I ring and leave a message. Several days later he dashes in just as we're closing and I'm trying to balance the till. He apologises for leaving it so late. I say it's fine and that Robert Frost is one of my favourite poets too, and he smiles as though that's somehow significant, already a secret shared.

"Perhaps if you're not in a rush I could buy you a drink for your trouble."

I'm taken aback. I've forgotten how to behave. But it's Friday and the children will be at Tom's.

We go round the corner to a dark Irish pub in Camden Road. There are a few couples on early evening dates and those trying to forget that they've nowhere else to go. A group of navvies sits staring morosely into their Guinnesses by the log effect fire. A middle-aged man in a sheep-skin, alone at the bar, is reading the sports pages. In the corner the lights on the fruit machine flash without much conviction. The place smells of stale beer and cigarette butts. There's a grey sadness about all these people putting off the moment when they'll have to go back to their cold lonely homes.

We struggle to make conversation over the amplified Ceilidh band, the general hubbub. Try to read each other's lips as well as minds. Robert Frost provides only limited mileage. He tells me his name is Liam. I ask what he does. He tells me he writes plays. Has had a couple on at the Bush and the Royal Court but the rest of the time teaches creative writing classes for adults. He asks me about myself. I decide to tell him I'm a photographer but not about the kids. I'm not sure what having a drink with a strange man means. I can't image that he'll be interested in anything I have to say, the things that overwhelm me daily. Tom's threats. My fear of losing the children. My yearning to take pictures, to find out where I come from, who I am. I feel uncomfortable and out of practice. It's easier to leave.

*

Scalter Street; Club Row, where once you could buy a pony from the gypsies brought in from Essex or Kent, bantams or a clutch of backyard hens, a mongrel dog. These days it's all cheap pet food and packets of unlabelled biscuits past their sell-by date. I'm beginning to feel at home in these streets, there's a sense of freedom I feel when out with my camera. It's as if I am beginning to see the world outside my head properly for the first time. To begin with I felt a bit threatened but now I'm beginning to relax, realise that I can simply be myself. That's the thing about the East End. It demands nothing of you. Outside the Turkish bakery a man in a long overcoat furiously addresses the air. In his arms he holds a battered teddy bear. What I see constantly surprises me, is far more startling than anything I could have imagined. How poor do you have to be to sit on the pavement and sell rows of broken shoes, old National Health specs, a battered transistor or a kettle without a lid? Who are your customers? From above her black veil, the kohl-rimmed eyes of the North African woman waiting outside the newsagents fix me with her stare. Her palms are hennaed. Orange whorls of intricate paisley. Far from her native sands and wide blue skies, what can she make of these narrow, dirty London streets?

Turkish, Urdu. Cockney. A snatch of Yiddish. Tongues I can't identify. A woman on an orange box sits selling good luck posies of ragged heather. One leg is normal, the other elephantine and swollen like something out of a Hogarth. The road is littered with broken vegetable boxes, squashed cabbage leaves and turnips. Muddy newspapers scud in the breeze. Everywhere faces are pinched with poverty. This is a place of ends and beginnings. The bottom of the heap. Here the mad, the bad and the dispossessed cluster in safety. It's a place to slip down to unnoticed, unkempt, unjudged or to climb out from by stealth or guile to a dream house with a tarmac drive at the end of the Central Line, in Ongar, Buckhurst Hill or Theydon Bois.

It begins to spit with rain. The stall holders hoick up their plastic covers which flap in the wind. An old man pulls a vegetable sack over his head. His face is the colour of putty, warty as a Jerusalem artichoke. I move out of his line of vision so he won't see me taking his picture. A huge woman, her bright orange hair piled in a bun on the top of her head covers the French knickers, the outsized satin corsets and lacy teddies with plastic sheeting. Over her jumper she wears a large brassiere to advertise her wares, wheezing and moaning all the time about the rain to anyone who will listen. It's hard to leave the market. It's like a drug. Maybe around the next corner there'll be the perfect shot.

✳

It's difficult to find his flat. The landings seem to go on for ever. I'm shocked by the cat turds. Not just one or two but the piles of hard chalky pyramids and steaming mounds in the corners of the concrete stairwell. I was completely taken aback when he phoned. He rang the shop. He only knew my first name. The lift is broken and graffiti decorates the walls like ivy. On the floor below his an abandoned sofa has been slashed so the springs hang out like entrails. Part of me is shocked at being shocked, that someone educated should want to live somewhere like this.

"It's cheap and there are no expectations."

I'm beginning to wonder if it was a good idea to come. And yet I knew I would. After we had left at the pub I thought that would be it, that I'd never see him again. I'd been so awkward. But I had thought about him. The thick untidy hair, with its odd thread of grey that makes him look vulnerable. The drawn Celtic face with the skin drawn tight across the bones. His slightly hooded eyes. My stomach is already churning. I know this is dangerous. A moth to a flame.

Taking a chance with what I know, deep down, will probably do me harm. An old feeling.

"Good to see you," he says, answering the door in bare feet. He's wearing jeans and a T-shirt, his dark hair's damp and recently combed back from his brow. He must have just got out of the bath.

The flat's small. More a studio bedsit. As if he isn't planning to stay long, to set down roots. A saffron and maroon kilim hangs on the wall between the book shelves. Papers, that minutes before must have been littering the floor, have been gathered into careless piles. On the bedside table is an alarm clock, a box of Kleenex and a tiny bronze Buddha. The poems of Wallace Stevens, a travel book on Chile. I feel embarrassed, as if these objects that make up his daily life are, without his consent, exposing too much about him. He kisses my cheek and, rather formally, offers to take my coat then goes and gets a bottle of chilled wine from his tiny cluttered kitchen. The duvet looks as though it's just been pulled hastily over the bed. I examine the bookshelves for clues into his thinking, his passions. Yeats, Joyce, Wittgenstein, The Tao of Physics. His desk is littered with papers, bits of script, an open thesaurus and I half notice, though dismiss it almost immediately, as though I had not glimpsed it among the mess, the photograph of a woman with long hair and a thin face. I wonder who she is.

I'm wearing long suede boots and a black calf-length skirt with small ivory buttons down the front, left open from just above the knee, worn with a heavy leather belt and man's cream silk shirt. I worried all day what to wear, changed twice. Didn't know what would appeal to him. On the way to his flat I kept checking my reflection in the bus window, the plate-glass shop fronts that distorted my image in their convex curves like those fun-fair mirrors that turn you into a midget or an elongated giant, squashing your head, stretching your limbs. I'd wanted to bring him something but didn't know what. Wine? I wasn't sure which one. A plant? In the end I bought olives. Green and marinated in thick Virgin olive oils and herbs in an earthen pot.

"Your hair. It was your hair I noticed first, Hannah," he says as his hands work out how to undo the tiny buttons on my shirt. "You have wonderful hair, like spun copper."

As he slips my shirt from my bare shoulders it slides to the floor, a puddle of cream silk. I'm aware of my dimpled stomach, the livid stretch marks turned to silver threads across my breasts, and wonder if he might be disappointed, if he wants perfection. But his mouth tells me otherwise. He has milky Irish skin. It has a blue sheen. There's the surprise stain of a birth mark around his left nipple. I trace my fingers silently across his chest, across the wine blemish as if trying to read Braille, decipher his history. I want to touch his bruised vulnerable places. We don't speak. We both know that I've come for this. We are trembling and the shadows from the gas fire stretch huge across the ceiling. Outside a train trundles past, going south, just outside the window, so I can't tell whether it's us or the room that's shaking.

All my senses are stretched. It's not just touch, his hands or wet tongue seeking out the unexplored crevices of my body. My whole skin absorbs the smell, the taste of him. His body is an uncharted landscape. I travel across its dips and valleys into the rocky cavern between his collar-bone and neck, to where his rib abuts sternum and groin meets thigh. Coarse hairs sprout from the dark discs of his nipples like ferns fringing the edge of a pond, run in a dark line down the thin white skin of his stomach from navel to matted pubis. On the rug in front of the blue of the gas fire, his hand lies on the arc of my hip. I try and freeze the moment. Pin it in the specimen case of my memory.

An oasis. Palm trees. A camel in a desert. I'll always think of these now when I smell his cigarettes. Outside the rain is beating on the corrugated roofs of bicycle sheds and boiler rooms. And through the thin walls, in other flats, I can almost hear the quiet pumping of other hearts; and beyond, the brown river flows silently past Butlers' Wharf, East past the ghostly remains of Deptford boatyards, converted warehouses and tower blocks, past the Thames barrier, to the sludgy estuary of mud flats where gulls circle and mew, and on into the sea.

✳

Yesterday was a heavy day in the bookshop. Everyone who came in seemed to ask for a book that wasn't in stock. I'm tired. It's Sunday morning and there's nothing to get up for. Blue-tacked over my bed is the poster of Piero Della Francesca's *Madonna of Mercy* that Liam bought for me in the National Gallery the first weekend we spent together. I can still see him, sidling up to me with it in a roll and slipping it, embarrassed into my hands.

"What's that?"

"For you. You don't have to have if you'd rather not."

When I got home I hung it up over the bed, and then, beneath the Madonna in her white snood rising in the centre of the painting like a giant column, her cloak outsretched in two huge wings to protect the kneeling fraternity of saints, we made love.

✳

I open the album. I've been thinking about it constantly as if it might hold the answer to some question I haven't even formed. I turn the black cardboard pages as if trying to read the future in the tea leaves at the bottom of a cup. Only in this case it is the past I'm trying to piece together.

46

Depth of field

Crouched on my haunches, my floral sprigged dress bunched into my lap, my sprung copper curls disciplined by a ribbon, I peer inquisitively into the bassinet, stick out a chubby finger and poke at the dimpled cheek of a bald baby. It's 1953. I am three.

"Say hello to your new sister Hannah."

"When's she going home?"

"Come on darling, don't be silly, you're a big girl now, she's staying here always. She's going to live with us. Soon she'll be big and be able to play with you. You're not the baby any more. Be grown up now and come and help Mummy with little Jackie."

"She's ugly. I don't like her."

A continuous flow of days seamed together in a haze of scrubbed teeth, well brushed hair and regular bedtimes. Maybe my own life is as much an invention as my parents' past. Did they, I wonder, ever forgive me for what I did to Jackie?

Perhaps that's when it started, the day they brought her home in that Moses basket, wrapped in a crochet shawl. This rage, this pain, compressed and black as coal. Premature, raw as a skinned rabbit, she screamed and screamed, the tiny opening of her mouth pink like the inside of some exotic shell, her lips trembling and blue from colic. I didn't want to be grown up. Why should I love her with her screwed up crinkled face and horrible cross cry? I never wanted her anyway. She was nothing to do with me. I just wanted her to go away and never come back. Maybe one day Mummy would take her shopping and leave her pram in the greengrocer's behind the potatoes and forget and come home without her. One morning, while she was sleeping quietly in her crib, thumb in mouth, I crept into her room and pinched her silky mottled thigh slowly between my thumb and forefinger until a flushed stain spread beneath the skin and she began to howl. Then I went downstairs to my mother, who was scrambling eggs for my lunch in the kitchen.

"Jackie's got a tummy ache, she's crying."

"What a sensible girl to tell Mummy. Let's go and give her a drink."

Is that when I learnt to pretend? To hide away my real feelings, because I wanted to push my sister's pram down the concrete garden steps or tip up her high chair on the hard tiles of the kitchen floor and smash that small bald head? I longed for it to go on being the same as before. Just me and them. And what if they could guess? What if they knew how wicked I was inside? If they could read my terrible dark thoughts?

It is sunny. Early June perhaps. Bees humming in the lilac. The sort of drowsy afternoon that so easily becomes gilded in nostalgia. The pulse of the motor mower throbbing through the orchard as Mr. Wicks cut the grass into neat tramlines on the far lawn, the smell of it, sappy and green, filling the thick summer air. Jackie is lying in her big black pram on the terrace near the fish pond, parked in the shade of the mock orange beneath a white fringed canopy. All pink and powdered, blowing tiny milky bubbles as she watches the shadows from the leaves form a jigsaw against the blue sky. My mother had left me making a miniature garden in a baking tin and gone to arrange the roses she'd just picked, in a cut-glass vase on the dining room table. The baking-tin garden had a real gravel path, flowerbeds and trees made from the heads of aubrietia and privet leaves. And a lake – the lipstick mirror borrowed from my mother's handbag covered with yellow ducks from the farmyard set.

I can still feel the dry earth pouring through my small clenched fist, through the holes in the cat net. See it trickle across Jackie's face, sticking in her shell-like ears, her eyes, clogging up her tiny rosy nostrils. On and on until I'd nearly buried her. After that I transformed my decorating skills to the cat net, weaving into its holes, daisies, leaves and grasses so that she must have looked like a Victorian baby prepared for a funeral bier or a tiny shrouded Ophelia. When I'd had enough I went to see if I could persuade the dog to lie still while I dressed her up in an odd assortment of clothes from the dressing up box and completely forgot about Jackie.

"Hannah, Hannah come here." My mother's screams split across the heavy afternoon, from the other end of lawn like the cries of a wounded animal. She'd come out to bring us in for tea. "Hannah, you are a wicked wicked girl. You could have killed Jackie." She was nearly hysterical holding a very muddy baby in a dirty white dress tight against her clean frilled pinny, trying to brush crumbs of earth out of her hair and eyes. "What were you doing? What do you think you were doing?"

"Just making her look pretty."

But Jackie had her revenge. She was an eczematous baby. At six weeks her skin erupted into a livid scarlet rash as if to spite me. It was as if her epidermis was a family barometer, a measure of my mother and father's parenting skills, a rebuke to their desired image of perfection. At night my mother would wrap her legs in gauze bandages, tie her scratching hands in white cotton mittens so she looked like a trussed chicken. Eczema, inflamed tonsils, she was always ill. They applied greasy emollients to her skin, cut out cows' milk, bathed her in special oils. I couldn't compete. Nothing I could do could grasp their attention in the same way. I could only sulk and be cross. Practise for my future role as the difficult one. Perhaps their anxiety was not just personal but cultural. The sense that at any moment they might be required to leave that wooded Surrey hill, that everything they'd acquired might be requisitioned and they'd somehow be forced to return to their rightful roots in Whitechapel.

※

Later I started to look for clues and signs. I explored the hidden places in the house which might yield up some evidence of a secret that I hadn't even named. I inhabited the dark space behind the hot water tank, high in the dust-filled eaves of the attic. I never let Jackie up there despite her pleading and she was too small to negotiate the rickety ladder unaided. I was scared of heights but it was worth it to be left alone without her always wanting to take my paints or Jack's. I hitched up an old tartan car rug in a sort of Arabian tent. It was there I kept my Derwentwater crayons, all neatly arranged in a tin with a lake on the lid. White through rainbow hues of pink, yellow and mauve, to blue and black. And the tiny glass bottle with a cork Grandpa had given me from Bournemouth, filled with layers of coloured sand. Special things. Private things.

The floorboards in the attic were rough and uneven. I had to be careful to keep to the joists, not to fall down through the gaps, through the plaster-board ceiling. But at least, up there, I didn't have my mother nagging me to be nice to Jackie because she was only little. Badgering me to take her down to the bottom of the garden to feed the rabbits old bits of lettuce. For as soon as we were out of sight of the house she would start to whine and moan, until the only thing I could do was to threaten to pinch her.

I felt an overwhelming sadness for all the discarded, forgotten things in my attic hideaway. A sort of anthropomorphic sympathy. The battered leather suitcases covered in luggage labels from Torquay, Nice or Juan les Pins that my mother's mother must have taken to the South of France between the wars. For the chipped sets of crockery and the wicker picnic basket fitted with green bakelite plates and matching mugs, strapped into separate compartments which we hadn't used since we went to Bognor for the day – when I was what, five? – and Jackie was sick in the back of the Humber. I thought how unwanted all these things must feel. I took them out and dusted and cleaned them lovingly, thinking they would some-how feel less neglected. The picnic basket must also have belonged to my grandmother. Not Grandma Millie, who lived in Golder's Green, but my other grandmother, Edith, who lived in a flat near Selfridges with a porter who wore a hat with gold braid. The one who one Christmas bought Jackie a doll in a cellophane box, with eyes that shut, and when I unwrapped my parcel and found an old handbag embossed with her initials, was furious, that I hid it behind the sofa, refusing to say thank you, so that I was banished to my cold bedroom and forced to spend the rest of Christmas afternoon alone for my rudeness.

It was in the attic that I kept my collection of marbles. I never took them to school. Never joined in the competitions in the playground. Sometimes I played Jacks, but was too cack-handed to bounce the rubber ball and catch it with the same hand. I collected marbles neither for currency nor exchange but for their swirling interiors. The deep blue seas, the dense glass-green forests.

In one corner, where the dusty cobwebbed eaves met the floor, was a collection of cardboard boxes filled with books, their covers yellowed and dotted with black spots of mildew. There was an ancient copy of *Lorna Doone* and the *Children of the New Forest* inscribed: *Rose Katz 1936*, cookery books with recipes for stretching war time rations. Recipes for Mock Crab made from a single tomato and egg, one for Rabbit Pudding: *Cut flesh of rabbit from bone into small pieces and add pepper and salt to taste. Line a basin with suet pastry and fill with the rabbit. Cover with pastry and greaseproof paper. Steam for 4 hours.*

Books on having babies: *Do not pick Baby up when he cries unless it is the designated time for a feed for you will create bad habits. Be firm. Start as you mean to go on. A well organised mother means a happy baby..... keep cracked nipples well Vaselined.*

Hidden at the bottom of one of the boxes was a book by Dr. Donald Hewitt M.D. – *Motherhood and the Newly Married Woman*. Between the musty pages was a series of line drawings. The sectioned diagrams made the expectant mothers' pear-shaped stomachs looked like boiled eggs with the tops sliced off. Inside was a tiny curled baby, small as the last one inside my wooden Russian doll, the one nestled in the middle that didn't unscrew. I didn't want to believe that babies really started off looking like frogs, with those enormous bulging heads. And what were that man and woman doing? *A woman may have to stimulate the man's penis manually...* I shut the book quickly. I didn't want to look.

I was still convinced that behind my ordered life of pressed viyella school shirts, piano lessons, tea at five o'clock, lay a darker more chaotic world. Sometimes when my mother was out and Mrs. Watson was cleaning the silver in a fug of cigarette smoke at the kitchen table, I'd creep up to my parents' bedroom and go through my mother's things hoping that I would elicit some hitherto un-revealed information. I was seduced by all the different pots on the kidney-shaped dressing table with its gilt mirror in three sections like a triptych and a frilled skirt I could hide beneath. I tried the block of waxy mascara by spitting on it and applying the black goo with a tiny brush, opened the china dish with its chrysanthemum shaped handle filled with fine face powder and a swan's down puff. In the wardrobe I found a fox stole. It had a black snout and glass eyes and lay curled next to a row of tiny veiled pill-box hats wrapped in tissue. I'd try on her collection of thin gold bangles, and practise tipping my arm so they ran tinkling up and down like a scale. I could always hear my mother coming before I saw her. In the nest of drawers between the twin beds I found a small book like a bible with strange writing inside that I couldn't read and *Masonic Grand Lodge* embossed in gold on the leather cover, a set of mother-of-pearl collar studs, a torch and a tube of cream beside a round pink tin containing a peculiar rubber dome. It had a strange smell. I shut the drawer quickly.

✳

There's a knock at the door. I'd planned on an early night. I slip my bare arms into the bat-wings of the willow-pattern kimono I bought to wear for Liam and belt it round my bath-pink body. It's Della. I'm rather surprised to see her. In one hand she's holding my bottle of witch hazel she borrowed, in the other, a bottle of Cabernet Sauvignon. She's wearing a black leather mini and a transparent chiffon blouse that maps the outline of her lacy underwire bra just above her nipples. Her ear lobes are heavy with gold hoops.

"Not disturbing you, am I Hannah?" she asks crossing the threshold uninvited. "Night off. Here, this is just to say thanks for the other day. Gotta corkscrew?"

I re-adjust the belt of my kimono and go in search of one, return-ing with two glasses to find her sprawled, under the *Madonna of Mercy*, on my futon.

"Cheers," she says raising a glass. "So what you think then Hannah, after the other day's little performance, should I leave him or what?"

It takes me a moment to follow her drift. I can't quite assess whether this is rhetorical badinage or if, for some reason, she's genuinely asking my advice. There's still a faint bruise, the colour of petrol on water, around her left eye, though her lip seems much better. Both are covered in a thick film of makeup. I'm rather taken aback.

"I've left him before but always gone back," she continues, re-arranging her body against my pile of Turkish cushions and exhaling smoke, with a sigh, through her nostrils. "Oh I don't know. It's complicated. See he's sort of family. Went to school together. Round the corner. Roman Road Infants. Always cock of the fucking roost. I've been with a lotta blokes, Hannah, but he's the best fuck. Electric dick I call him. Hard to give that up!"

I smile at her candour and make myself a roll-up. She seems set to stay.

"Sorry. No offence. Know I'm a bit crude. You see," she adds without waiting to be asked, "something sort of keeps making me go back. My Mum were the same. A string of useless fellas," she says pouring herself another glass of wine. "What they say? Like mother like daughter? Didn't know my Dad. Went to the Scrubs when I was four. Never came round after that. Well my Mum was with Harry by then. So I s'ppose he just drifted away. Heard once he was in Marbella. Should have brought you some proper fags," she nods disapprovingly in the direction of my straggly roll up. "Here have one of mine," she holds out a packet of *Marlborough Lights*.

"I'm fine thanks. Prefer these. Means I smoke less."

"Her and Harry was always fighting. I remember, as a kid, shutting myself in the toilet in the yard behind the washing line. The fence ran right along the railway track. My brother kept rabbits.

54

He's a mechanic now. Funny the things you remember. His Y-fronts and Mum's flowered apron flapping in the wind. The thuds and screams and then the sobbing and pleading when he threatened to leave her. Swore I'd get myself a nice quiet insurance salesman. Never found one that turned me on though, did I?" she says, her face breaking into a knowing smile. "Do you know what I'd really like – sounds wet doesn't it? – but a cottage in the country, you know with roses round the door and a couple of kids. When I was little I had these two cactus things. Won them in primary school for the best Tables Test all term. Kept them alive for ages. Like two prickly dicks they were." Her laugh is infectious, deep and chesty. A smoker's laugh. "I think it would be nice to grow things. Sort of sense of achievement. But Dave would think I was half-baked if I said anything like that. So what you think, then, Hannah?"

"I'm not sure," I say taken aback by this uninvited revelation "that I'm exactly in a position to give anybody advice. Anyway it's not really my business. It's not as if I'm such an expert on relationships myself, but if he's threatening you, perhaps you should just get out. Refuse to get involved, play his game. Something like that. It's really up to you."

"And what about you Hannah? You got a bloke?"

"That's a bit of a long story. Two. Well not at the same time. I was married for quite a while. Then I got divorced and moved here and now there's sort of another guy. A writer, but I'm mostly busy with the kids and work."

Apparently satisfied with my inconclusive answers, she tips back her straw blond head and drains the dregs from her glass. The upward curve of her throat is white against the line where her make-up finishes. There's something poignant about the partial revelation of the face she's painted over, like the sudden discovery of a private vulnerability when one secretly pokes through someone else's bathroom cabinet and finds a haemorrhoid preparation or a packet of condoms. She gets up and deftly slips her stockinged feet into the patent stilettos she kicked off across the room when she came in.

"How's the photography then? That's what you said you do isn't it? If you don't do it for magazines, what you take then?"

"I take pictures of the streets. Round and about. I've got this big exhibition soon. I've still loads to do."

"People interested in that are they? Funny. I'd prefer to see a bit of glamour myself. Had a bloke come into the club one night. He was a photographer. Girlie stuff. He made a bomb. Made me an offer. Said anytime I was interested I should give him a bell. Always jetting off somewhere. Nice work if you can get it. What you do when it's your time off?"

"Not much nowadays. Read. Go to the odd film. But mostly I work."

"Well I won't keep you. Can see you're ready for bed," she says straightening her leather skirt. "Better let you get some beauty sleep Hannah. Forget we have different clocks. Only dropped in to say thanks for the other day, be neighbourly like, now we've met," she says letting herself out. And as she closes the door, the smell of her expensive perfume does not leave with her.

❋

April 30th 1959. The photograph is torn but inscribed underneath in my mother's hand in black ballpoint. It must have been taken on my eighth birthday, the day I got my first box Brownie. The one with a canvas case and a strap so I could carry it over my shoulder. Here in London, over thirty years on, I hold the crumpled image of my parents standing next to the blue hydrangea by the front door and can't believe so much time has passed. More than half a life. That during all those years, somewhere, out there, unknown to me, both Tom and Liam were growing up. That there

56

was no Josh, no Annie. Everything seems so arbitrary, so based on chance. Perhaps we are unable to believe in the past, in what we have not experienced directly, except as a sort of myth. Photographs provide us with something tangible. Evidence, that like doubting Thomas, we can touch and feel.

The picture is blurred and over-exposed. A dark smudge fills the left hand corner of the frame where I forgot to move my thumb. Jackie is sitting on her tricycle beside my father who is, as usual, smoking his pipe. My mother wears flat sandals, a navy spotted shirtwaister with a white cardigan slung over her shoulders and has a tense anxious look on her face. She looks so young. I can't remember taking it. Until then I had only ever had a home-made pin-hole camera. Mrs. Jennings had shown us how to make them in General Science, how to cut a hole in a shoe box, blacken the inside and tape aluminium foil over the opening which we pierced with a pin and covered with opaque tape. It seemed like magic. Pictures from an empty cardboard box. I created arrangements of apples on the dining room table, dressed up the dog and made him sit still on the loggia. But they all came out the same ectoplasmic blur.

Carol, my friend from down the road, was three years older than me. She had given me a Ladybird book called *The Young Photographer* and a packet of little gold paper corners to fix snap-shots into my album. Carol's hair was cut in a bob and her thick brows met across the bridge of her nose. She had smooth olive skin. It wasn't until years later I realised she looked like Frida Kahlo. I loved her with total dedication. She was the source of all knowledge. I didn't know how I'd ever catch up, come to know all the things she knew. The names of all the English Kings, my Nine Times Table. She lived with her mother who was house-keeper to a retired civil servant at the Court House. His wife had died, so her mother did everything. Sometimes we would see him sitting on the terrace by the French windows just above the fishpond, a tartan rug over his knees, a gold monocle round his neck on a black cord, bent beneath a helmet of silver hair, reading, or occasionally pottering in the green house among the asparagus ferns. He didn't take much notice of us, sometimes calling us over to offer a boiled sweet from an inside pocket of his battered jacket. He'd been in the Foreign Office. In Alexandra. Though I didn't know where that was at the time. After his wife died he'd stayed on for a few years, though he was already retired, to study Coptic desert sects. The Court House was dark. Behind the door was a stand for walking sticks and umbrellas made from an elephant's foot and on the hall table an aspidistra in a copper pot. The oak panelled walls and bureaux were covered with small Egyptian figurines with broken arms and legs and flat-faced 13th century icons. Carol and her mother lived mostly in the kitchen and in two tiny attic rooms on the top floor. Her mother wore long coloured beads and tied her hair back in a paisley patterned scarf. She'd been an actress. She seemed, to me, exotic, with her dark rich voice. I was a bit scared of her. She was divorced. She'd been married to a painter. I had heard my parents whispering that he drank. Nobody else I knew had a mother who did anything except look after them, go shopping and get their fathers' dinners. No one else had a mother who was divorced. Carol said they were poor. She said it defiantly like an accusation. It made me feel guilty as though it was somehow my fault. I wondered if she minded. One day my mother had given her mother a bag of old clothes. She was always telling me off for my extravagances. It was a waste of food to cut crusts off bread, she said. Yet when the next tea-time came and we were seated at the kitchen table washed and ready for the fish-paste sandwiches her mother had made us, and I diligently made a point of eating my crusts, she'd later invent another rule.

"You don't need to use more than two pieces of paper when you pee," she'd say, waiting at the open doorway of the green tiled lavatory behind the scullery, while I sat with my serge knickers dangling round my ankles. I longed to please her. To show her I wasn't, as I suspect she thought, profligate.

I don't know who took these other pictures of my birthday party. My father perhaps. Because it was my birthday, we were allowed to bake potatoes on a bonfire at the bottom of the garden. Here we are collecting dry twigs from the orchard and laying them in a wigwam over scrunched balls of newspapers as we had been shown to do in Brownies. Carol was a Sixer and had her survival badge so knew how to blow the fragile red embers until they sparked the kindling. We wrapped the potatoes in silver foil and buried them in the ashes until the outsides cooked black, though the insides were hard as nuts. We ate them with dollops of butter scraped straight from the paper. They tasted of burnt earth. We sat round the fire and invented stories of shipwrecks and desert islands. A world somewhere between *Kidnapped* and *Swallows and Amazons*. I was always a Princess and Carol a Prince. We knew we would be rescued by a passing pirate ship so weren't worried. It was a game we often played. We knew the rules. I never wanted to be the Prince because I got to wear Grandma's old blue taffeta evening dress from the dressing up box. Carol didn't mind. In fact she preferred it because she could wear the opera cloak with the bronze lining and tell me what to do. I never saw any necessity to query the arrangement.

We weren't sure what to do with Karen. My mother had insisted I invite her. She and her mother, Joan, were friends. They'd met when my mother joined the committee for the School Choir Fund. My parents thought Karen charming with her soft foxy ringlets and clear thin voice. All the teachers liked her.

I didn't think she and Carol would get on. Carol was different. My parents talked of her as 'poor' Carol. They included her in things because they felt sorry for her and thought her intelligent, that she deserved better. "...so hard on the child. Apparently, though, *he* comes from a very good family..." Karen arrived in a pink nylon dress and white ankle socks. We were in shorts and sandals. She didn't like making bonfires she said. Though she did have a potato, carefully separating the pale centre from the charcoal with her fingers. Carol thought she was stuck up because she kept fussing about getting her dress dirty and wouldn't join in when we played hobby horses which was our best game. All our horses had names. Daisy, Buttercup, Silver, and were made from my father's old socks stuffed with laddered stockings and tied onto lengths of broom handle Mr. Wicks had cut for us. They had boot-button eyes and darning wool manes and halters made from shoe laces. We held gymkhanas in the orchard under the apple trees, setting up jumps and awarding ourselves rosettes if we managed a clear round. God! what do I look like. There I am waving, pretending to be Pat Smythe, cantering through the long grass with the fluttering ribbons held between my teeth.

"I don't understand. What am I supposed to *do*?" Karen sulked, refusing to play, and spreading her white cardigan under the apple tree so as not to get grass stains on her best dress.

"It's a stupid game anyway," she said belligerently, "jumping over sticks and pretending to be a horse. What's the point? I want to go home."

Carol and I had our own special place deep under the canopy of matted rhododendrons at the bottom of the Court House garden. It was down past the vegetable patch, past the rows of rancid brussel sprouts and bean poles covered with the dry tendrils of last year's scarlet runners, past the steaming compost and the potting shed, the seed trays and cracked flower pots. Right in the centre, where the shrubs grew thickest, was a hollow. It could only be reached by lying flat on our stomachs and pulling ourselves crab-like on our elbows through the tunnel of branches. On Sunday mornings, while my mother was cooking the roast beef and my father dead-heading the roses, we had our secret camp there.

"I'm getting scratched. Look I'm bleeding."

"Hannah you do make such a fuss. You're always fussing about something. There are people in Africa who are starving, who never have enough to eat and you're complaining about a few scratches."

I would bring my comics. *Girl* and *School Friend*. But Carol didn't think much of comics. They're for people who don't know how to read books, she'd say.

"I know how to read a book."

"I don't mean literally. People who haven't got the stamina."

"What's that?"

"Oh never mind. Anyway the *Eagle's* much better. I don't know why girls always have to have second best."

Carol brought her *Collins Book of Garden Birds* stuffed into the pocket of her shorts. She was mad about birds. She knew the names of them all. Nuthatch, wren, great tit, willow warbler. The colour of their breasts and tail feathers. I only knew which were blackbirds and robins. One Sunday, sitting in our hideaway, a bag of sherbet lemons bursting against our tongues, we started to talk about babies. She said she didn't want to have any, that she wanted to be an artist. I said I wanted six.

"Do they come from kissing?"

"Don't be stupid Hannah. Don't you know anything? The man puts his willy thing, inside the woman."

"How?"

"The woman has to touch it. It goes all hard and long."

"Ugh," I said, shocked and disbelieving. But she was never wrong about anything, about the names of birds or the dates of the Tudors, or how to do fractions.

"And before that a woman has to start bleeding. She does it every single month. It comes out of the same hole the man puts his thing in. You have to stuff cotton wool up it."

"Look," she said standing up, lifting her tartan kilt and pulling down her navy-blue knickers "they put it in here." I watched amazed, as her index finger parted the soft folds already sprouting a few dark question marks of hair.

"Does it hurt?"

"Only the first time. It's supposed to feel nice. But I think it's rather silly. Any way if I don't want any babies I won't have to do it. Are you sure you want six now?"

I hoped when I grew up I'd never have to do anything so terrible. I'd never seen a naked man. Except in those pictures in the attic and Mrs. Watson's little nephew. She 'did' for my mother and had brought him to our house once when her sister was in hospital with her nerves. He'd wet his pants and had to borrow a pair of Jackie's knickers. All he'd had was a tiny pink knob.

I was afraid someone would find us, though no one knew where we were. I couldn't take my eyes from her parted legs but she pulled up her knickers and brushed the earth from her skirt as if she'd simply explained another fact that I was too stupid to know about. But the image of her finger disappearing inside her slit kept slipping back into my mind as I soaped myself in the bath. Presumably if Carol looked like that, I would too one day. My mother did. I'd caught a glimpse of her dressing one morning through the crack in the bedroom door.

All week I looked forward to Sunday but often, when it arrived, I couldn't wait for it to be Monday again. Usually my Grandpa Dan and Grandma Millie came to lunch but, invariably, it made my mother cross. She clattered baking tins and busied herself basting the joint and roast potatoes, stirring Bisto into the juices and sighing while the wireless played *Two Way Family Favourites: This is for Ron stationed with BFPO forces in Germany from his fiancée Shirl in*

Chelmsford. Love you always. See you at Christmas.

I liked Grandpa. He did magic tricks, pulling a silk handkerchief in mid-air out of my ear. For my birthday he gave me a brown ten shilling note and a white leatherette jewel box covered in pink roses. Inside the lid a tiny ballet dancer pirouetted round and round on one leg in front of a mirror. It had a brass key so I could lock it. Annie's got it now. Though she broke the dancer when she stole Josh's Dinky car after they'd had a fight and tried to lock it inside, so now the dancer is stuck in an endless motionless arabesque.

✳

My Grandma was small and bird-like. She wore little shiny high heels and always carried a matching handbag and had a clean white hanky stuffed up the sleeve of her cardigan, just-in-case. She dyed her hair but pretended she didn't. "It's not ladylike Ma. It's much more elegant to go grey," my father would repeat exasperated each time she visited. But it remained ink black. An uncomfortable reminder that his acquired good taste had not been inherited. Each morning she had a cold bath, scrubbing herself with a loofah and a piece of rough cloth. "Good for the circulation. My Ma always did it. Wasn't no hot running water in Whitechapel in them days and she had perfect skin when she was seventy."

She always brought her own food. Cold fried fish in greaseproof paper, pots of chopped liver and fat warty cucumbers in vinegar, *gefilte* fish. My mother snapped and grew short tempered. Perhaps it was because Grandma wouldn't eat what she'd cooked. Not the meat anyway. It made her even crosser when she tried to give my father a piece of cold fried fish.

"Go on son, it'll do you good."

"Jack doesn't need that, mother, we've got roast beef."

And my father, ignoring them both, would poke at the roast beef

63

on his plate with his fork, making the pink flesh ooze a river of red juice, like someone prodding a dog in the road to see if it was dead, and grumble.

"This is underdone. You know I can't eat beef if it's raw and these aren't the right glasses for claret, Rose."

And she would answer that it wasn't raw but rare, as the corners of her mouth bunched into tight little creases, and that she wasn't cooking a good piece of Scotch beef to a cinder.

Then my father's face would cloud as he reached past me with an exasperated sigh because I'd forgotten to pass the gravy.

"Hannah do pay attention. Why don't you ask if anyone wants anything? You'll have a husband to look after one day and you won't find one with an expression like that."

Sometimes at night I would creep along the draughty landing and listen outside my parents' door. I thought I might understand why they always seemed so cross. Perhaps they'd get divorced and I'd end up poor and having to live in someone else's house like Carol or worse still have to go to an orphanage and wear other peoples' cast-offs. At Christmas we always cleared out our toy cupboard and packed up the things we didn't play with any more, and the clothes we had outgrown, for Dr. Banardos. My mother told me it was important to think of those less well off than ourselves. She'd pack up the car and take the cardboard boxes to somewhere in Battersea. Perhaps I'd hear my parents talking and learn that they didn't like me as much as Jackie because I had been adopted and wasn't their real daughter.

I stood on the dark cold landing holding my breath, trying not to breathe. The moon was low in the tall black firs at the bottom of the garden. My feet frozen against the polished lino as I shivered in my flowery nightie. If I stood there long enough I might even hear them doing the thing Carol had told me about. But there was only ever the hum of the hot water in the radiators. I couldn't really imagine them doing it as they slept in different beds. That would mean one of them would have to climb into the other's and there wouldn't be room. Anyway I'd never even seen them kiss or hold hands.

The cross feeling often lasted until Monday morning. I thought if I kept quiet, didn't say anything, it might go away. I'd slip downstairs hoping my father had already caught the 7.15 to Waterloo, but he'd still be in the dining room, a crisp white napkin on his lap, eating his toast and marmalade behind the *Daily Mail*. He kept *The Times* for the train.

"Good morning Hannah," he would say offering me his freshly shaved cheek.

I knew he expected me to say good morning first. To kiss him. Why did he always wait to be kissed? It was the same in the evening when he got back from the station. He would come through the door, put his bowler hat and umbrella on the hall stand, and pour a measure of malt whisky into a crystal tumbler. I knew he was waiting. And something obstinate and hard began to grow inside.

I had forgotten about the piano. Only half of it is visible in this photograph of the morning room. How could I forget when I spent so many hours there staring at the wood panelled walls or struggling with the B flat minor? I can't imagine who took it or why. The room is in half-shadow. The light, pale and wintry, coming through the French windows from the garden. There are the photographs of my father in uniform on the mantelpiece. A bowl of roses. The dog curled on the rug. Suddenly I can hear Miss Kandinsky's voice. "Hannah you vant to learn to make music. You must do proper practice." But I wanted to get out into the garden to meet Carol in our rhododendron hideaway where we met to eat our elevenses.

"What's it like not having a father?"

"I *have* got a father. It's just he's an artist. Artists aren't like other people. They don't like to be tied down. They need to be free to think. To be creative. He lives in a little cottage on the beach on the Isle of Arran. Hardly anybody else lives there except some fishermen," she said dunking her digestives into her orange squash. "A boat comes twice a week with the post and newspapers. If it's too stormy they can't get across."

I knew that sometimes she received brown paper packages from him, done up in sealing wax and string. Drawings of birds. Plovers, curlews, even a golden eagle. She had them pinned on her bedroom wall. Her love of birds seemed to be a way of staying in touch with him.

"When I grow up I'm going to live with him. I'm going to be an artist too. I'll collect mussels from the rocks. You cook them in wine."

"Have you ever been there to see him?"

"No, but I will. Soon. I'm going to look after him."

"Won't that be boring? Having no one to play with?"

"Intelligent people don't get bored. The best will be before breakfast. I can do what I like there. He won't mind. I'll borrow the binoculars from behind the back door and go and sit on the rocks and watch birds. They come across the North Sea. If you're patient there might be something rare. Ornithologists go there."

"What're they?"

"People who study birds. Then I'll go back for breakfast. He'll make me porridge. Real porridge with salt."

"Salt?"

"That's how they eat it in Scotland. It has to be cooked in a pot on the stove and left over night. There's no electricity. They use candles and water from a well. You have to do everything there. He makes his own bread. We are going to get a goat for the milk. I'm going to learn to milk it."

"Can I come? Can I have a go?"

"Maybe," she answered with obvious reluctance "but I don't know if he'll like you though. Not if you bring your comics."

"If I don't bring them, can I come? Can I?"

"I suppose so. I suppose we could go next Saturday."

"How will we get there?"

"How do you think silly? We'll walk."

"But what about sleeping and food? How long does it take to walk to Scotland?"

"We'll take provisions and blankets. We'll sleep in haystacks and barns and cook on fires in a black pot hanging from a wigwam of sticks beside the hedgerows like Romanies. We'll bake hedgehogs in clay and forage for nuts and berries and mushrooms in the clearings under the beech trees. It'll only take about three days if you keep up with me and don't lag. You can't come if you moan."

"I won't, I promise," thinking this was not the moment to mention the hedgehogs.

I envied Carol her father. He seemed much more interesting than a real one.

Everyday after tea we met. Not under the rhododendrons because we were in school uniform and didn't dare get dirty, but at the back of the potting shed. We made long lists in a small red household accounts book Carol's mother had given her to draw in, full of useful information about how many furlongs made a mile and how many quarts made up a pint.

Saucepan. Sugar. Tea... Carol wrote.

"But I don't like tea," I said.

"Well it's too bad unless you want to do all the carrying. We can't take too much. Have you got any money?"

"Five shillings in the Post Office Grandpa gave me for passing my Grade III piano."

"Bring that then. For emergencies."

Sugar, String... she continued writing.

"Nine o'clock then. At the potting shed. Don't forget your torch."

That night I listened for my mother's footsteps as she went down stairs. Eight-thirty. She'd just said good night. I crept out of bed and pulled out my satchel from the back of the wardrobe. Torch, hot water bottle, sugar, a packet of chocolate Bourbons stolen from the larder. Two apples. Some elastic bands and a ball of string. I picked up my latest copy of the *School Friend*, then put it back reluctantly on my bedside table, my heart pounding, as I pulled my thick jumper over my pyjamas. Dressing gown, wellingtons. I was ready. It was still not dark outside as I crept downstairs so as not to wake Jackie as I knew she would tell, and out of the backdoor and down the hill towards the Court House potting shed.

It was Mr. Wicks who saw me. From the top of his ladder where he was mending a gutter at the back of the house. I can still see my father standing at the top of the hill bellowing "Hannah. Hannah come back. Come back here this minute."

But I never sneaked. I never told on her. I just kept insisting that I'd had a bad dream. I never said that it was all her idea or what we had meant to do. It wasn't until the next day that I learnt that she had been in bed all the time. Had never been at the potting shed, had never made any preparations. No torch, no string, not even the tea. Perhaps it was at that moment that I understood something of betrayal, that dreams and reality were not the same thing.

"It was a game. Just a game, Hannah. You didn't think we could really walk to Scotland did you?"

We didn't play together much after that. Carol was busy working for the Eleven Plus. She got a scholarship. Then she and her mother moved to be nearer the grammar school. I didn't see her again. It wasn't until years later that I started hearing her on the radio, seeing her name in *The Observer*.

✳

Leaving the cottage in Somerset had been a form of major heart

68

surgery. Dismantling the kitchen like severing the main artery. Once it had been the hub of the house. Now the pictures had been removed and the drawings the children had brought back from play school, thick with sludge-coloured paint – *'it's a tractor; it's you Mum,' 'lovely, darling, you are clever'* – had left smeared patches on the walls streaked with wood smoke. The dresser stood empty, stripped of its rows of chutney, jams and jellies. The dusty herbs had been removed from the beam above the fire. The wood stack was empty. Kneeling in the middle of the floor, wrapping everything in old newspaper, I kept discovering lost objects, like forgotten appointments in an old diary. The silver fish knives we received as a wedding present from my aunt, those horrible African mats Tom's mother had sent when they were stationed in Nairobi.

"Hannah, Tom's so good with the children," my parents had said after Annie was born, forgetting they'd never wanted me to marry him, impressed that he should make up bottles, hang out the washing.

He tried, I suppose, in his fashion. After all it hadn't been much of a childhood, his father's regiment always overseas in Gibraltar, Singapore, Rhodesia, with his dappy, sandy haired mother in tow, smelling of Yardley's lavender water and knitting for the church. Intricate little matinee jackets "for those poor little coloured babies".

I was shocked, after we had been sleeping together a week, wedged in that narrow bed in his digs that smelt of cat piss, trying not to make a noise because Mrs. MacShane didn't allow girls, when he confessed how he had sobbed under the bed clothes in the dormitory so the other boys wouldn't hear. Always terrified of waking to a soaking mattress and pyjamas, to the humiliation of cold water and a bar of coarse soap. It was the only time I ever saw him cry. He turned to the wall so I wouldn't see his tears. His naked back a cream curve in the moonlight.

They all went home for the holidays to their bikes and gardens, their pet rabbits and little sisters. "I was always shipped off to some aunt I didn't know. There was always," he added bitterly, "an endless supply of spinster aunts with floury skin and bad breath."

His mother's letters would arrive regularly in elaborate looping script covered in foreign stamps. *It's too expensive Tom-Tom to fly back for only four weeks, but we are absolutely longing to see you, darling in the summer!!!* There was always a full regiment of exclamation marks. As if life was simply a pleasant game. A continuous round of understated polite behaviour. He was only eight.

Perhaps that's when he invented perfect parents, constructed an ideal family he never saw, to be brought out like a photograph from his wallet, in front of the other boys in class. A defence against being teased.

"My Uncle's a big game hunter, he's shot hundreds of tigers and my father has thousands of men in his battalion and drives a tank."

"Don't believe you."

"He does. I tell you he does."

I don't know how I came to have this photo of Tom. It must have got mixed up with my things when we were sorting out the house or maybe he gave it to me and I can't remember. He must be 13. There he stands, slightly out of focus on the station platform at the end of the school term: long knee socks, shorts, and elastic belt with a serpent clasp, his leather suitcase and the Beano, like something out of a 1950s *Picture Post*, as the other boys are collected by mothers smelling of Ponds Cold Cream and fathers in felt hats and brogues. He is peering through those terrible pink-rimmed National Health glasses for the right platform number for Hove or East Grinstead. He was half-blind even then.

I think of all those forlorn holidays he must have spent collecting tadpoles in jam jars from stagnant ponds behind the bamboos in small suburban gardens. Or sitting quietly in a silent mahogany breakfast room with his stamp collection while his aunt was out polishing the brass in the church. For a treat, a bachelor uncle, all tweed and nicotine yellow, might come and take them for a spin in the car, a visit to a stately home. Dark, full of armour and large dingy paintings of stags and cherubs. Or they might drive to Bexhill, away from the crowds and park by the sea-front to drink their thermos of milky tea (sugar in a twist of brown paper) and eat *Rich Tea* biscuits as the rain lashed the promenade and white sea horses beat up against the beach. If he was lucky he'd be allowed one ice cream as long as he didn't drip it in the car. There were never any other children to play with.

✳

At first Liam is reluctant to spend too much time at my place. He's concerned about becoming too attached to the children and they to him. I have been having trouble with Josh. I had a call from his year head the other day asking me to go to the school and see him. Apparently Josh has been skipping lessons and going with Buzz and Sam to the park. The CDT teacher was on his way home the other afternoon and found them smoking in the bandstand when they should have been in Maths. At first Josh denied it until he realised that the school had told me. On the whole it's easier to go to Liam's place when the kids are at Tom's, it avoids split loyalties and complications. Often Liam works when I'm there, at his desk in the window that looks over the railway. So I've been sorting out his room, organising the piles of books alphabetically, the fossils, the bits and pieces he brought back from his travels in Nepal and the Far East. The bronze Buddha, the set of temple bells which I strung along the mantelpiece. I unpacked his life from the boxes where it seems to have remained for years as if he could never make a commitment to living anywhere in particular.

71

"Hannah, you're amazing. This place looks twice the size."

When I stay with him he brings me breakfast in bed. Already showered and dressed he comes in from the tiny kitchen with a tray laid with a white cloth, a pot of steaming coffee, plump croissants oozing butter. He is good at the little things. His body, food, sleep, for once all my senses are satisfied. After we make love I curl naked inside his large sweater inhaling the scent of him and snuggle back under the duvet drifting in and out of sleep listening to the pop of the gas fire as he does his marking. He resents that. Not the teaching. He loves the chance to talk about books, but the time wasted when he could be working on his play.

I am beginning to understand something of the nature of work from him. I find it hard. He seems simply to lose himself. I can't do that. I am always anxious, about the children, how things are going with Tom, whether he really loves me. He never says.

But slowly I'm beginning to discern a theme in the photographs I am taking. At first I wandered the streets randomly taking shots of whatever caught my eye. I spent a lot of time trying to guess which was the house my father grew up in. Whether it was one of the ones that has recently been bought by a developer, or one of the many sweat-shops crowded with Bangladeshi women bent over treadle machines making cheap clothes for *Top Shop* and *Etam.* I don't know exactly which street it was in. It's something I've never been able to ask. It's as though my father's past has simply been erased and with it my history. I've walked up and down all the small roads that run in between Commercial Street and Brick Lane. Quaker Street, Hanbury, Princelet and Fashion Streets. I know that it was in one of these that my grandfather had his workshop. They lived in the back. My grandfather wanted my father to become an apprentice, a stone setter, like him. "If you have a trade son, you'll always have something to sell." But my father didn't want to be a jeweller, to spend hours in a freezing workshop up three flights of stairs bent over a low wooden workbench setting precious stones under a paraffin lamp. As soon as he could he left the grey tenements filled with the flotsam and jetsam of Europe, the dank, rank yards where lousy children played tag and skipping; the shoemakers, wachmakers, cigarette makers, the tailors, the tarts and their pimps, left the narrow lanes that echoed like a dark threat to the discordant voice of Mosley and his blackshirts. In the pictures I take I want to achieve a certain quality of pensiveness. To touch the viewer with a sudden stab of recognition, one that somehow arouses a tenderness for the subject, which if passed in the street would not even be noticed. It's not the freaky quality of Diane Arbus I'm after, but something closer to pathos. Sanskrit has a word for it: *tathata*. It means: *Look, there it is, that's it!* It's a moment of recognition.

I keep browsing through books on the great photographers. I suppose if I'd gone to art school and not married Tom I would have done more of that, had more of a confident basis from which to work. I am entranced by Stieglitz's *The Horse-Car Terminal. New York 1893*. The horses' breath freezing as it hits the cold air, the white snow in the city streets turning to slush. I know that it's early morning. Can feel the cold in the bones of the cab-man in a long coat with his back towards me. I try to imagine a life without photographs. No records of the small rites of passage, of birthdays or that afternoon in Eastbourne when it blew a freak gale or the Girl Guide outing to the New Forest in that May heatwave. No evidence of a life. Just a blank. Like celluloid exposed too long to the sun. Whited out.

And when I'm not looking at Stieglitz or Cartier Bresson I return to my own green-calf album. I am drawn back and back. It's as though my real life is to be found there. It's these photographs I dream about.

✳

Brown blazer, striped tie, felt hat. My leather satchel bristling with rulers and pencils. I'm standing in the left-hand of the picture by the spotted laurel outside the school gate, staring awkwardly at my shoes.

"Just one photo Hannah. Your first day at big school," my mother had insisted. I was embarrassed. Didn't want to be marked out as a new girl.

I can still smell the chalk and beeswax polish. See the mots of dust dancing in the sunlight. The pools of gold and vermilion bleeding onto the stone floor from the stained-glass windows. The heraldic griffins and lions passant shadowed on the rosewood panelling. And all around, like the suck and hiss of the sea, the rise and fall of girls' voices.

Our Father who art in heaven, hallowed be thy name...

I wanted to let go. To drift off on the downy current of sound.

Thy kingdom come, thy will be done...

Every day the same. School notices, prayers, then a hymn:

Father lead us gently lead us o'er the wide tempestuous sea...

If I shut my eyes really tight, their voices sounded like sirens in the wind. I thought I would faint. I wondered if I concentrated hard enough, if I'd feel God's presence, but our Scripture teacher said He only came to those of a meek and humble heart and my mother was always telling me that I was moody and difficult.

If only I could have prayed. I tried. I really did, but I didn't know how. No one ever explained what I was supposed to do. I would empty my mind, concentrating on the diamond pattern of my Start-rite sandals, hoping to squeeze out the thoughts that kept swimming into my head. But there was always the boiled cabbage from the kitchen or the rings in the arm pits of Sandra's viyella blouse to distract me. Sandra who wouldn't use deodorant because she said it clogged the pores. And then there was Karen. She never prayed because she was Jewish.

"My parents have written a letter. I've got special permission. We don't believe in Jesus, so I can't pray to someone who's not there can I?"

And she would casually loop up a stray foxy curl, watching for the effect of her carefully calculated words. While the other girls mouthed their prayers she would sit hands folded, lips pursed, still as a stone effigy on a Victorian grave. I didn't know what it meant to be Jewish? Did she also agonise whether *Science and Health* by Mary Baker Eddy was true, whether illness was a judgement for lack of Faith. She didn't seem concerned about being at a Christian Science school. She knew she was only there because it was the best in the county and because her father had moved from St. John's Wood in order to set up his firm of solicitors. She knew she was Jewish and would one day leave and marry a wealthy Jewish husband. Maybe the Christian Scientists were right. All you needed was faith and God would protect you.

Is that why he didn't protect the Jews? Because they'd lacked faith, failed him as his Chosen People? I felt paralysed by what I'd seen. The enormity of it. I'd known nothing. Nothing. I'd never meant to watch, never meant to look. But they came back again and again in the middle of the night, those flickering shadows I'd seen by chance, late on television one night when my parents were out and thought me in bed. Terrible haunting pictures that made me afraid to walk upstairs in the dark, afraid even of the sound of my own breathing under the heavy eiderdown. Pictures I tried to pretend I'd never seen. Of bodies, piles and piles of broken bodies with bones poking through bruised leather skin and limbs tangled like the spiny branches of felled trees. Men and women with shaved heads and dead-fish eyes in striped pyjamas, sitting blankly behind barbed wire. Stick people. Thinner than I believed it possible to be and still live. If I'd been born in a different place, at a different time, would that have been me, Jackie or my parents? For I knew that I was somehow connected to those grey ghosts. Huddled in my plaid dressing gown, the room lit only by the coal fire, I couldn't look, couldn't turn away. Was that what it meant to be Jewish? To live in the heart of nightmare?

Maybe it was comforting to be a Christian Scientist. Even though after nearly a year I still didn't really know what they did. I knew they didn't believe in doctors but if I asked one of the boarders to explain they said there was no point, that I wouldn't understand. Why wouldn't I? I knew they couldn't take aspirins if they had a headache and had to sit in the Quiet Room and read the works of Mary Baker Eddy. That if they were really ill they went to a Christian Science practitioner who sat with them and prayed. I had heard girls whispering about relatives who'd died rather than see a doctor. Maybe they simply hadn't had enough Faith. Being ill was all in the mind, they said. You could decide to be well if you really wanted to.

Give us this day our daily bread and forgive us our trespasses as we forgive those who trespass against us....

"Oh dear God, please, please forgive me for being so bad tempered and coming downstairs in a dream and forgetting to say good morning to Daddy at breakfast. I didn't mean it, honestly I didn't. Please make me good, make me whatever it is they want me to be and I really promise, or I hope to die, that I'll never doubt that you exist again."

I felt ashamed. Jews were forbidden to say the Lord's prayer. Karen had said so. I was a Jew, at least a sort of a Jew. Though no-one had ever said so exactly, so I couldn't be sure. It was just something I'd begun to acknowledge like the unbidden changes in my body. My family wasn't like Karen's. She took time off for Yom Kippur and Pesach. I didn't even know what they were, but I felt guilty all the same. I stopped praying in assembly. My family never talked about being Jewish. Just as they never talked about my father's childhood in the East End or my mother's Aunt Dot. The one they found wandering on the Epsom Downs in her petticoat. The

76

one who smelt of camphor moth-balls and rose-water. I had heard their hushed conversation one evening as I was sitting on the stairs, just out of sight, while they drank their after-dinner coffee.

"Better off... can't cope... asylum... danger to herself... can't be expected..."

I never really knew what had happened. Years later, I pieced together the words instability, electric shock, spinster, into an approximation. I often thought of her, pale as bath-water, wandering round the grounds of that red-brick Victorian asylum in a faded summer dress even in the middle of winter, chewing a hank of thin hair in the corner of her mouth. Her days spent basket-weaving, sitting in a lavender and urine scented day-room staring out across the uneventful lawns, her stockings rolled around her ankles, as the other inmates did giant puzzles of the *Mona Lisa* or sat round like children, taking part in the enforced jollity of a sing-song. There had been talk of a married man. Something had, it seemed, gone terribly wrong. I wondered if such conditions could be inherited?

I think I would have liked to believe in Jesus, even to have been a Christian Scientist. In primary school I loved the picture of him in the Scripture corner, dressed in blue surrounded by small barefooted children with black, brown, yellow and white faces, a halo shimmering around his long curls. There he stood with his beatific smile bending, with his hands outstretched, to bless them as white doves fluttered over his head. At Christmas we had a nativity table covered with straw with plaster statues of Mary, Joseph and a shepherd carrying a lamb. One year I was allowed to make the gold star.

I didn't know Jews weren't supposed to eat pork. "It's unclean," Karen whispered, in the lunch queue behind me when we had bacon casserole. I didn't know what she meant. But I just had greens and mashed potato to be on the safe side.

One Friday, after school, she invited me to her house. I was nervous because I thought that she'd think I'd know what to do. Gold-rimmed china dishes full of chopped liver, sprinkled with parsley and hard boiled egg were laid on a white cloth beside silver candelabra. There were lace napkins and a plaited loaf covered with poppy seeds. Her father said prayers. He wore a skull cap on the back of his head held on with a Kirby grip. Like a picture I'd once seen in *Punch* of the Pope. I'd never heard Hebrew before. Sweet wine was passed round the table in a silver cup. I didn't know I was supposed to take a sip.

Why did Karen's family do these things and not mine? We didn't have any special feasts. At Christmas we gave presents and had a Christmas tree. I saved my pocket money for weeks. At the gift counter in Woolworths chose between packets of lemon bath salts and a manicure set in a leatherette case for Grandma, nail clippers and *Imperial Leather* for my father. Every year I had a different colour scheme. Purple tissue and silver bows or black shiny paper tied criss-cross with gold ribbon. Everybody else just did theirs up in robins or snowmen. I kept mine hidden until the last minute, so Jackie couldn't copy. Then stacked them under the tree in front of the heavy red velvet curtains in the bay window of the dining room.

I loved the tree, the sense of continuity it gave me. The same old decorations rescued from layers of dingy yellow newspaper. The cardboard and cotton-wool stars made in primary school. The glass balls like frozen icicles and the fairy with real lashes and silver spangles on her wings. Each year she appeared a little more tarnished, a little dustier. I'd creep downstairs when everyone was in bed and the house silent, apart from the noise of the hot water pipes and the dog snoring by the boiler, and sit leaning against the banister, my nightie tucked under my knees, watching the lights flicker green pink and red.

Holly and paper chains. The bustle in the shops as long queues formed at the International Stores for dried fruit and baked ham,

78

while girls at the marble counter, their hair in turbans of net, slip-slapped butter into quarter and half-pound blocks with wooden spatulas and the butcher sliced slivers of bacon onto the white tiles. Every year the same argument "Hannah's greedy, she's got a bigger spoon, she's eating it all," as Jackie and I fought over the enamel basin streaked with egg, brown sugar, the dark traces of cinnamon.

On Christmas Eve there was sherry and hot mince pies with the Wentworths. I'd never taken much notice of Stephen. Sometimes I'd glimpse him cycling up the laurel-lined drive on his racing bike but then he was sent off to Stowe. That holiday, as he sat at the piano accompanying our carols, his heavy fawn hair kept falling over his glasses. He seemed different to the boys at the tennis club. I couldn't stop thinking about him and made him a hand-painted card and slipped it between *In the Bleak Mid Winter* and *Oh Little Town of Bethlehem*. But he never mentioned it. Not even when I saw him on Boxing Day at the Trocodero.

We always met there for lunch. We drove up to London, my mother in her silk two-piece, smelling of Chanel No 5, sitting in the front of the Humber. Jackie and me in our best woollen dresses with velvet collars and patent Princess shoes in the back. "How much longer? Are we there yet? I feel sick." Regent Street and Piccadilly glimmering. The head waiter greeted my father – he expected to be remembered from year to year – and led us to a table in front of the four piece orchestra, in white tie and tails, playing Strauss and Ivan Novello. Plush red carpet. Crystal chandeliers and gilt mirrors. Banks of silver cutlery covered the starched linen. The head waiter flambéed chunks of meat on a sword at the table and an Indian in silk pyjamas, turban and golden Ali Baba shoes served hot curries and something called Bombay Duck which my mother whispered was not duck at all "but a sort of disgusting rotten smelling fish that they eat in India". Then came the sweet trolley groaning with trifle, junket, sherry chocolate cake...

...and lead us not into temptation...

Was it hypocritical to pray with the others? Would God mind if I said the wrong prayer? Karen sat silent and assured, as the elastic of my beige socks cut behind my knees. I thought of our R.E. teacher, quiet and disapproving, as she explained how Catholics tied bits of rope around their waists under their clothes as a penance.

"So theatrical the Papists," she sniffed.

Once I put blotting paper in my shoes before assembly. A girl in my class had said it drew the blood and made you faint. Maybe then God would hear me.

Strange how things bubble up in the memory. I'd completely forgotten the day I burst into the kitchen while my mother was making Charlotte Russe for a dinner party, and throwing my satchel down on the chair, asked "What religion are we really Mummy?"

She didn't look up, but went on listening to Mrs. Dale's Diary, whipping the cream in a fluted china dish.

"Oh I don't know, sort of C of E I suppose," she replied scraping clean the sides of the bowl, wiping the edge of the knife on her rose-sprigged piny, "Now hurry up, wash your hands, tea's ready."

"Then why do we never go to church?" I asked her back which was already disappearing into the pantry.

...for thine is the kingdom, the power and the glory, for ever and ever, Amen.

✳

When it came, I was too embarrassed to tell my mother. I was all peony flow. All body. I was afraid of its brightness, its otherness. I thought of Carol's dire warnings under the rhododendrons. Only months before, my mother had come into my bedroom to 'talk to me'. I can still see the awkward angle of her body, silhouetted in the early evening sun, as she balanced on the pink satin eiderdown of

80

the narrow nursery bed I still slept in. I was reading *Little Women* for the umpteenth time.

"All grown up women get The Curse. You simply have to learn to put up with it."

She was quiet. Matter-of-fact. As if explaining the details of the Green Line bus time table or how to boil an egg. I wondered how Jo, Beth and Amy had managed. I couldn't look at her face and lay pretending to count the rosettes Carol and I had made for our hobby-horse gymkhanas, that were still pinned round my bed. First. Fourth. Highly Commended. After Carol had moved away I never played that game anymore.

For two days I said nothing. Simply stuffed my white under-knickers with scratchy Bronco toilet tissue, pulling up the navy regulation ones over the top to keep the blood-soaked paper in place. Ashamed, I prayed no one at school would stick a head over the top of a cloakroom cubicle and discover my secret. I longed for the end-of-lesson bell. Sitting beside me in French or Biology, could they smell? The paper was too shiny and tell-tale trickles ran down my legs drying into a chocolate crust. I couldn't concentrate. In Science we were doing amoeba, spirogyra and asexual reproduction. Long chains of green looping cells ribboned across the page of my text book. Outside the lab window, leaves from the copper beech swirled in the damp autumn mist, forming a ruby carpet on the lawn. The room smelt of rubber and formaldehyde. I wondered if this was a form of damnation.

From the blackboard I copied: *Protozoa the lowest and simplest of animals, unicellular forms or colonies multiplying by fission.*

Miss McPhee had labelled all the parts of the diagram in her neat crabbed script. As she wrote I couldn't take my eyes from the dark shadow on her chin. There were the rumours that she had to shave everyday like a man. I had never seen her wear anything except the same hand-knitted grey cardigan and neatly pressed cotton blouse, held together by a small Victorian silver brooch that spelt 'Agnes'. And when she sat on the dais, at her raised desk in front of the class, you could see right up her skirt. She sat with her legs open and wore long pink bloomers elasticised at the knee. I wondered if Miss Agnes McPhee bled.

My body was erupting into peaks and tufts. Its familiar pink smoothness was betraying me. I was slowly becoming someone else. Someone I wasn't ready to be. One afternoon after school, when my mother thought I was outside on my bike, and Mrs. Watson was putting sheets through the mangle in the back scullery, I shut myself in the garden lavatory. No one used it except Mr. Wicks. My mother didn't like him coming into the kitchen with his muddy boots. She even took his tea into the garden in a big white mug she kept specially for him so he didn't have to use ours. The panes in the small window were cracked and feathered with cobwebs. The sill filled with old seed trays and broken flower pots sprouting shrivelled marigolds and dried begonias. A spare bicycle wheel hung rusting on the wall. On the floor, hidden behind the stained lavatory pan, was a muddy magazine full of women with blond hair, huge bosoms and no knickers. I listened for footsteps, then wedged the handle of Mr. Wicks' bicycle under the wooden latch. I'd crept into my parents' bathroom and stolen the scissors from my mother's manicure set and my father's Gillette razor. Slowly I snipped and scraped at the bed-spring curls sprouting between my legs until tiny berries of blood appeared and I looked like a plucked chicken.

Changing into our airtex shirts and box pleated shorts for hockey, I noticed Karen and Sally sniggering as they wriggled their small snail-white bodies out of their chill-proof vests. I didn't want breasts. I hated the feel as I ran across the playing field, the thick straps of my cotton brassière cutting into my shoulders. When the captains picked members for teams, I was left until the one before Lynette, Lynette who had blackheads and never cleaned her teeth. Then

Miss Barrett put me in goal and made Lynette stand out as a reserve until half-time. I didn't care. I stood there for nearly fifty minutes, my knees raw in the February wind, then missed the only ball shot in my direction.

Life became a series of locked doors. Chill bathrooms. Soaking and rinsing dark stains from my white knickers. Pools formed like melting glaciers on the polished linoleum beneath luke-warm radiators. But the brown rings wouldn't wash out, stayed imprinted like the age marks of felled trees. And Jackie was always there. Outside the bolted bathroom door, knocking and moaning because I wouldn't let her in.

"I've got to clean my teeth. Mummy said so. Hannnah, let me in, why can't I come in?"

One morning, before school, my mother found four wet pairs dripping behind the hot water tank.

"Hannah? Have you started The Curse? Why didn't you tell me? I told you to come and tell me."

I said nothing. Pretended I hadn't heard as I counted the rosebuds on the bedroom wallpaper. I hated the word. It gave me the creeps, made me think of witches, of filthy secrets. Why were women cursed anyway? What'd they done? I didn't want anything to do with it. I just wanted to be me.

She led me into the bathroom and locked the door. Then from the back of the glass-fronted medicine cabinet, from behind the bottles of Friars' Balsam, Vicks and Cod Liver Oil, took out a bulky paper packet marked: Dr. Whites no 1.

"Now take your knickers off and put this on. Like this."

She held up a pink elastic belt with an adjustable hook front and back, and from the packet pulled out a bulky gauze sanitary towel with cotton loops on either end.

"Open your legs."

"Now these. They'll stop leaks getting on your clothes," she said handing me a pair of pink nylon knickers with a thick rubber gusset.

"And don't forget, make sure you wash yourself thoroughly down there when it's your time-of-the-month. You don't want to smell now do you?"

✳

My skin, my hearing and vision are becoming more receptive. When I walk down the street I see black against white. White against black. Things are continually measured in perspectives and depths of field. Separate moments framed. An old man with a whippet by the canal, his vaseline skin etched with deep tracks of pain, a gang of West Indian boys with thick-soled trainers and baseball caps sitting on a wall, the wires of their walkmans trailing round their necks like exotic jewellery, chatting up two young girls, one in sawn-off denim shorts, the other in a tiny black lycra skirt with lemon leggings.

At first I wasn't sure if it was just my imagination. I thought that the building next door was empty. But it's been going on all morning almost out of range of my hearing like something dreamt. Broken cords, phrases and arpeggios, played over and over again. Ghost music. And my mind slips back to that cold music room. The heavy anaglyptic wall paper, the piles of yellowing music and the cats. Most of all to the smell of cats.

"Hannah why you waste my time? You don't practice, you don't learn. Why you bother to come to lessons if you never work for me ugh? You want to be ordinary?"

Miss Kadinsky's voice was sad, pleading. As if I'd let her down.

Smaller than most of her pupils, her wild steel hair tamed with inappropriately girlish bows and ribbons, she always wore a flowing chiffon scarf. I think she wanted to look like Isadora Duncan. She

84

was the first artistic person I'd ever met, except for Carol's mother. But she had moved away when I was nine. Miss Kadinsky fascinated me with her thick Russian vowels, her deformed fingers ending in stubbed crimson nails painted to match the inaccurate bow of her red lips. She could barely still stretch an octave. Her arthritic legs had, with age, become too bowed to reach the pedals. Yet sometimes, as I climbed the narrow cat-scented staircase, I could hear her doing battle with the chords of Tchaikovsky's piano concerto, like someone attempting to bag an unruly ferret.

"Ah, Hannah when I was young. How I could play," she would tell me over and over again. "I was only 16, still at the Paris Conservatoire, when I was invited to give a recital for the Conte d'Orleans. It was my début. I wore an oyster *crêpe-de-chine* dress and fresh lilies-of-the-valley in my hair. They all fell in love with me, Hannah. Oh how they fell in love. The Conte sent me a dozen white roses. And the jewels, Hannah. Ah, the jewels."

"And did you ever go back? Home. I mean to Russia?"

But she would turn away, her faded egg-white eyes weighed with sadness.

"A concert pianist. I should have had a career as a concert pianist. But then you know," she would sigh, changing the subject "there was the Revolution."

Now she made a living teaching the piano to girls who rarely showed either enthusiasm or promise. Often when I should have been doing harmonics she would tell me how she had played in the bars and cafés of Paris. Reeled off names. Braque, Picasso, Satie. Names that meant nothing to me. Sometimes, lost in afternoons drinking tea at the Café Flore with Stravinsky or Sunday mornings rowing on the lake in the Bois de Boulogne, she would forget my scales. Other afternoons she would be eating ices by the bandstand, under the horse chestnut, with the handsome violinist from the Conservatoire. I longed to be part of such an exciting, romantic world.

She inhabited two attic rooms at the top of a shabby Victorian house. Her companions three huge unneutered Toms. They ruled her life, draping themselves across the lid of the upright piano, spraying the cluttered parlour with their penetrating musk. There was something, I realise now, heroic about her, wandering Europe with nothing more than a gift for music and a tragic flawed optimism. Who knows what she'd seen, what horrors she had suffered? I don't know if she ever married, ever had children. How could she have foreseen, as a young protégé playing Rachmaninov in Moscow, that she'd end her final years teaching colourless English girls arpeggios?

Her walls were covered with dingy religious paintings in mahogany frames. Small icons of doe-eyed Virgins, encased in silver, hung above the horse-hair sofa. Flat Byzantine faces gazed in blank adoration at the Christ-child with his wizened old-man's face. Along the top of the piano, faded women in large hats and high-necked blouses with cameo brooches clasped at the throats, smiled from a row of sepia photographs. Two small boys in knickerbockers and Eton collars sat in a pony trap, their arms around a Great Dane. In another, three young girls wrapped in bonnets and fur muffs, skated on a lake. At its edge a brass band played. I never dared to ask who they were or what had happened to them. Everywhere books and piles of music were turning yellow, gathering dust.

I knew I should practise. I wanted to please her, earn her praise. But I hated the ugly sound I made. It depressed me. It had been in that room, on her wind-up walnut gramophone, that I'd first heard Beethoven's *Moonlight Sonata*. Through the crackles I knew I was hearing a new language beyond anything I'd yet experienced or understood.

"Hannah again you haven't learnt the F sharp minor. Why are you so stubborn? You have real feeling for music, a gift, but it's no use without you practise. You make me angry."

Sometimes I imagined telling her. I longed to confide in someone. I wanted to tell her that the music was trapped inside, that I didn't understand theory and hated the endless routine scales. That each time I sat down to play my fingers tripped over the keys producing a travesty of the sound I heard in my head. Often before school, I'd sit in front of the piano in the icy morning room, staring at the passepartout framed photographs of my father in his RAF uniform on the panelled walls above the fake log electric fire, in a rage of anger and frustrated tears. How could I admit to her that I couldn't manage it, that I didn't have the stamina, the patience. That the only talent I had was for feeling.

I knew my father wanted me to play. It was one of those female accomplishments he valued. For perhaps, in secret moments alone, he regretted where his life had led him. Once out of the blue he told me he'd wanted to be an engineer, to build bridges. Perhaps he blamed my mother for not being adequate compensation. And my mother blamed him for blaming her and for not understanding that it was not done to eat your roast beef burnt and for not knowing all the things she thought, when they married, he would know.

Frozen silences. I longed to exchange my bush of wiry hair, my heavy limbs for Karen's curls and apricot skin. But I couldn't play for him. I had to protect us both from that disappointment.

"Hannah you're getting spots," my mother said. I was getting fat. At night I crept downstairs, across the cold tiled floor, to cut wedges of fruit cake from the tin in the larder, picking out the translucent glacé cherries in the dark.

※

Sunday lunchtime. Washed hands, combed hair. I sat in front of the hunting-scene place mats, the silver rose-bowl of friesias, hoping they wouldn't notice. As Jackie gabbled on about her

87

homework, I kicked her under the table for taking the last roast potato, with a glare in her direction, daring her to squeal. She squirmed but said nothing.

"Hannah do stop scowling and help your mother clear the table. Try and cultivate a bit of charm. You'd do as well to take a leaf out of your friend Karen's book. She's a delightful girl, speaks beautifully. Did you know Rose," he said turning to my mother, "her father is about to be called to the bar?"

After we had dried the plates and my mother had taken in coffee and cream on a tray to the lounge, she told me to go and practise. In the cold morning room I opened the piano and began a Chopin prelude. It was one of the few things easy enough for me to play without having to sight read. I played it over and over again, my fingers fluent for once until, finally exhausted, I slammed the lid shut. I wouldn't play anymore. What was the point? Next lesson, I decided, I would tell Miss Kandinsky I was giving up the piano.

※

I am walking up Roman Road towards Bethnal Green when I bump into Della. I've never seen her in the street before. I've just been at the gallery discussing the exhibition. It's terrifying, there seems so little time, so much to do. We stop and chat for a moment and then I invite her for a coffee in The Cherry Tree, at the Buddhist Centre.

"Blimey, you think they'll let me in," she jokes good humouredly tugging down her short leather skirt. "Not quite me all this healthy living," she says as I come back to the table she's found in the window next to the notice board covered with leaflets for Hatha yoga and massage, Tai Chi and meditation, with our coffees. "Well what you up to then, Han? Haven't seen you around. You're a sly one. I saw that bloke of yours leaving the other morning early. He looks all right."

As she chats she pulls out a pink copy of *Loot* from her large gold holdall bag and announces, much to my surprise, that she has decided to leave Dave, to move out and find a place of her own. She has finally put her foot down she says, told him she wouldn't put up with any more of his messing. She has already circled several of the advertisments in red felt tip.

"How about this one? *Fourth professional girl wanted to share large house on the edge of park. Own room, near tube. Phone Veronica after 6.00pm.* Sounds a bit posh for me, Veronica! What about *Self contained bedsit near London Fields. All mod cons. £65 per week?* Think it's a good idea Han?"

"I think it's brave, Della. Will you really do it? It's hard living alone," I say finishing my coffee and wondering why on earth I'm allowing myself to get involved in something that has nothing to do with me, as I hear myself announcing, "I've got a spare room. You could always keep an eye on the kids."

✳

Fifteen. There I am fifteen and all I want is for him to notice my dress. It's French blue with sprigs of white gardenias sprinkled across the skirt and three layers of net petticoats, almost strapless, with only bootlace ribbons to hold it up across my bare shoulders. I am wearing it for the tennis club dance. It is held each year at the Grange Park Country Club. Built between the wars it had once been a private house. The halls are long and tiled and our high heels click as we walk down them admiring ourselves in the long ormolu mirrors. There is an air of seedy grandeur. The small lounges, on either side of the ballroom have faded little pink velvet sofas and banquettes arranged around small gilt tables. In the corners are large dusty potted palms. At the end of the hall is a small pool with a marble statue of a naked nymph with an urn on her shoulder pouring water into the pool. The marble is yellowing and slightly cracked.

I am standing by the bar with Karen. She is wearing her mother's best rabbit bolero stole. Her dress is shiny eau-de-nil taffeta, a scoop neck with a pale lemon sash around the waist. On her feet she has silver peep-toe sandals. I can't remember who the boy is who's standing beside us holding up a glass.

Karen was the tennis club star. She was county standard. Everyone wanted her for a partner. She played to win, running across the court stretching for even the most impossible backhands, her blond ringlets caught in a ponytail bouncing pertly behind her, her pink cheeks shining. I hated tennis. I didn't care enough about winning. Instinctively I shied away from competition. I never expected to be better than the next person. But my mother insisted.

"Now listen Hannah, if you improve your game you'll be asked to join in the mixed doubles."

My mother thought I needed to get out more. That I needed some new friends. That way, she said, I'd meet a nicer type of boy. She didn't approve of the ones from the grammar school who hung round town on Saturday mornings, hair slicked into Elvis quiffs, cigarettes drooping from the corner of their artfully curled lips. She liked Stephen Wentworth who lived next door. He was going to Cambridge. Once, when I was much younger, I'd made him a Christmas card. But he took no notice. Anyway I didn't like him anymore. He only ever wore a tweed jacket with leather elbow patches and his school tie even in the holidays. And he played the piano all day. I hadn't time for that any more.

But I liked Jeff. He used to hang around with the other boys, I noticed, when I went shopping with my mother and Jackie. One afternoon I saw him up at the club. He didn't seem the sporty type. I thought he'd like jazz and foreign films. But he was just there to collect tickets for the dance. As I came out of the changing room he was lolling against the bar, the collar of his jacket turned up, wearing dark glasses. His skin was cratered with acne scars but I couldn't stop thinking about him.

Three girls and three boys. Karen, me, Stephen Wentworth and a friend of Stephen's from school and Karen's two cousins, Howard and Jane. Howard and Jane had come down from London and like Karen were Jewish so went to dances in St. John's Wood and Finchley. Jackie sulked all day because she wasn't allowed to come – my mother said she was too young – so she hid my bottle of *Pink Pearl* nail varnish I'd bought specially on Saturday morning in town at the back of her knicker drawer. We piled into Karen's father's Jaguar, flattening our stiff net petticoats to make room. The boys wore their father's ill-fitting dinner jackets, their smooth hair wet with Brilliantine and shiny as their patent leather dance shoes. The band played *Living Doll* and *She Was Only Sixteen* while little groups sat at small tables sipping fruit cocktails from tall frosted glasses under a net of coloured balloons. Across the polished dance floor couples shuffled at arm's length.

"No cheek-to-cheek nonsense now," warned the ample-breasted Mrs. Crowther from beneath her corrugated perm. Mrs Crowther ran the club dance every year and watched vigilant as a hawk, waiting to strike down any inappropriate intimacy as couples plodded round the room – *and a-one-two-three-onetwothree* – the hours of ballroom dancing in the school gym etched onto their souls. She had crooked teeth smudged with lipstick and her thick powder gathered like dust in the deep creases of her face. Huddled in the four corners of the room, bleating and giggling, small groups of girls tottered on white stilettos.

All afternoon I'd been locked in the bathroom shaving my legs raw, squeezing blackheads in the Radox steam. On the clouded mirror I'd written *Hannah loves Jeff*, forgetting when it misted over again the letters would return again to betray me to Jackie.

91

"You look like a shopgirl from Woolworths," my mother snapped when I emerged, my head a porcupine of pins and jumbo rollers. Woolworths seemed to form something of water-mark for my mother's social aspirations.

"What *are* you doing?" she continued, following me back into the tropical bathroom where I was dunking a net petticoat into a bowl of liquid sugar.

"It makes them stiffer. Everybody does it."

I could see him across the room. Thin black boot-lace at the neck of his pleated shirt. His tuxedo too closely fitted round his narrow hips to have been borrowed from his father. His dark glasses poking from his top pocket. Suddenly he started to walk across the room towards our table. He stopped. My heart leapt. He was going to ask me to dance. But instead he invited Karen. Now only Howard and I were left as the others were all on the floor. He asked me to dance. It was a fox-trot. I was grateful. He was not very tall and beneath the shadow of a moustache, the gaps between his teeth were filled with calcified tartar. He manoeuvred me stiffly with a hand in the small of my back like someone learning to drive. I didn't know what to say, what to talk about. He went to school in London and was, he told me, going to join his father's firm and become a solicitor. Then the music broke into a Cha Cha Cha and he delivered me formally back to the table and went to get a drink. I was trapped and alone. I didn't know how to leave the table so just sat there holding my empty glass and smiling and smiling until the muscles in my face ached. Karen was at the centre of the dance floor with Jeff, a confection of taffeta bobbing up and down to the Latin steps.

The whole room seemed to be staring. Oh dear God, please, please make Jeff ask me to dance. But neither God nor Jeff seemed to hear. Even dancing with Howard was better than this. I wanted to go home but couldn't leave until Karen's father came at midnight. Across the room Jeff was now dancing a waltz with Karen. Her long foxy curls were wound softly around her head in a loose chignon. So close, he was holding her so close, his head bowed towards hers so their foreheads were nearly touching. I wanted someone to hold me like that. Quietly I got up and slipped into the cloakroom to re-adjust my suspenders, to secure and re-secure the pins that held up my French pleat. I needed something to do. The bright lights over the big white hand basins showed every blemish and spot that seemed to be erupting on my skin. I stayed there as long as I could backcombing, pinning and dampening my kiss curls until the attendant sitting in her white starched apron at the door started to give me a frosty look and I had to slip 6d into her saucer. I didn't want to go back but I couldn't stay in the cloakroom for the rest of the evening.

The lights dimmed. The band was playing a slow smoochy number. Above the dance floor a ball of tiny crystal mirrors revolved in a spotlight, spangling the dancing couples in fractured snowflakes of light. I huddled in the darkness against a radiator hoping no one would notice. I could see Jeff pull Karen closer, watched his tongue playing with a stray curl over her left ear.

Tell Laur-a I lo-ve her.

I wanted to go home.

"You want to dance Hannah?"

It was Howard. I was overwhelmed with gratitude. I didn't care about the hair on his lip, his yellow teeth. At least I wouldn't have to stand jammed against the radiator. As we took to the floor I could feel his vinegar breath on my face. I didn't want him to hold me so close, but was anxious, after he had asked me to dance, not to seem rude. After a quickstep that neither of us could do, he took my hand and led me into the room where they had hung the coats. It was cold and dark. He didn't say a word as he pushed his tongue like a floundering wet fish into my mouth until I thought I would choke. I hadn't expected kissing to feel like that. But I was grateful that I wasn't sitting alone watching the others dance. Rough tweed chafed

93

against my bare shoulder as he pushed me further and further into the curtain of coats, fumbling with the bows on my shoulders, peeling back the whaleboned bodice of my evening dress like the skin of a grape. His hands were rough and dry as he plucked and pulled at my nipples. I didn't know what to do. What was expected. Neither of us spoke. Is this what other people did? Was this what Jeff would do with Karen?

Outside the band was still playing.

Tell Lau-ra I love her.

Howard's hand was over mine so I couldn't pull away, his breath coming in short stabs, his full weight on me. Backwards and forwards, backwards and forwards. The open fly buttons, the damp sticky hair... *the woman touches it to make it hard...* I could feel it like a broom handle prodding into my stomach beneath my dress. It smelt musty like rotting mushrooms. Frozen, I closed my eyes waiting for him to stop, trying to pretend I wasn't really there as his eyes became glassy, and his lips parted, pulled back over his teeth. It was only my body, after all, crammed between the heavy overcoats, my mind was elsewhere, a blank. Then suddenly he gave a shudder and dropped my hand. I looked down and saw a damp stain had darkened the front of my dress.

Karen's father came and picked us up just after midnight. The others piled laughing and joking into the car. I was crammed in the back beside Howard who spent the whole journey flicking bridge roll crumbs at Stephen. I wanted him to put his arm round me, to take my hand in the dark. To make it all right. But he didn't speak to me at all. Not once.

Changing Apertures

When Liam stays with me in Bethnal Green, he gets up early before the children. We are both wary of creating routines and exceptions. If they are with Tom or my parents for the weekend, I stay with him. Sunday is a rumple of newspapers, stained sheets and warm skin, crumbs licked from navels and breasts. My face buried in the hollow of his armpit. Home.

I notice a number of guide books in his flat. Books on Greece. The *Guide Bleu* and *The Rough Guide*. I ask, trying to sound nonchalant, if he's planning to take a trip. I know his half-term break is due. I had hoped he might spend it with me. If he's going to Greece I want to go too. But I'm too embarrassed, too uncertain of his response to ask.

"Yer, I need a break. I'm brain dead. Sucked dry with teaching. I need to unwind before I get back to the play."

"When are you going?" I ask trying to sound as casual as I can. I don't want to appear demanding.

"In three weeks. Come if you want."

The children are with Tom and Alison for half-term. They have decided to take them on the Broads, think that they need some fresh air in their lungs living in London. But even so I'm a bit nervous about what they will make of my going off to Greece, if Tom will try and use it against me in some way. But I don't want to stay in London alone.

We catch a boat from Kimi, and head north. Liam never likes taking the easy route. He has to feel as if he is travelling, not walking like one of those pond flies on the surface, never penetrating a culture. He'd travelled so much in the past. Greece was the place he went after he left Belfast at 18. It was the first time he'd been outside Ulster. He simply got on a ferry, held out his thumb and travelled down through the spine of Italy, the blue hills of Umbria, past mountain top villages with terracotta roofs and black cypress trees inky against the horizon, to Brindisi, then across to Piraeus. He'd travelled round the whole of the Peloponnesus. Stayed in barns, slept in hay ricks, stealing grapes from the vines for his breakfast, working for a few nights washing glasses in a bar in an island port. Old women mothered him. Offered him damp figs from a basket when he passed them in the dusty road. Bread. A bed. He was a good linguist. Picked up Greek easily. As the boat heads east, a shoal of dolphins attaches itself to the wake leaping the wash like a group of playful teenagers showing off to the delight of the passengers crowding to photograph them from the deck. We settle ourselves in the corner by the life boat and lay out our towels. Liam reads Miroslav Holub while I sunbathe, my head in his lap. I absorb it all hungrily like someone starving, the pleasure of the heat, his large hand absent mindedly rubbing suntan oil onto my back. This is happiness. A blue arc of sky. This moment stretching on into an infinite future.

When we get to Skyros we take a bus to the far side of the island. We ask in tavernas and shops selling lace and leather sandals for a room. A small boy points down a whitewashed alley to some steep steps up the side of an unfinished house. We follow him up to a room on the roof. A carved double bed. Cedar, with a traditional design of Skirian doves. A marriage bed ready for his sister's wedding. On the balcony a scribble of geraniums spills from a blue painted oil drum. Smells of pungent basil. And from the window, the brown hills curve behind the shimmering bay. Beneath the steps is a tiny washroom that opens out onto the street. There is a single tap and a cold shower. Liam strips off his sweat soaked T-shirt, his dusty shorts. We stand under the shower and I cover his hair with lather, watch the soapy water drip from his pubic hair, leave snow-capped peaks on the port-wine island on his chest. He winds a towel around his hips and climbs back up the steps. A trail of wet footprints, toes and heal, is left imprinted in the dust across the marble floor as I follow him upstairs my hair wrapped in a towel.

He is more relaxed, more himself than I've ever seen him. As though snorkelling naked among the rocks, among the striped angel fish and spiny sea urchins can wash away the deep pain of Ulster that lies ingrained beneath his skin and to which I know he will return again and again in his play. As he tans the blue veins in his hands seem to disappear. We read and eat. Grilled mullet. Greek salad with a dribble of olive oil and feta cheese. Walk across the island through the blue pine woods, down a dirt track, past small farmsteads and gnarled silver olives, past a group of goats munching at the spiny scrub, to a deserted bay.

We visit Rupert Brooke's tomb. "Imagine," he says, "the ignominy of being a war poet, the golden-boy of your day and dying, not at the front, but after being bitten by a mosquito. Now that's bathos." We spend an afternoon looking at rugs and knick-knacks. He buys me a silver ring entwined with two dolphin. The days slip by.

✳

Two blank pages. One still has three of the transparent paper corners. The glue has turned the colour of ear wax but the photograph has disappeared. The next few are covered with drawings in thick felt tip. A dove. A peace sign in gold paint. Garlands of flowers intertwined between a collage of newspaper cuttings.

Loudhailers. Mounted police. Students with flares and head bands, rucksacks and duffel coats. From Scotland, from Cambridge, from Bangor. Neat sandalled Quakers, yellow robed Buddhists, communists carrying red banners emblazoned with the bearded profile of Che Guevara swell the street like a flood tide. Decimation and violation. Deforestation and genocide. Dishonour and shame. Vietnam. The sound of *Blowing in the Wind* scatters like petals into the crowd. A girl, her eyes, two kohl-dark pools in the tundra of her face, carries a single rose.

What do we want? NIXON OUT OUT OUT!

When do we want it? NOW NOW NOW

It's strange, but I see now, as I go through the album, how often the small highlights in my own life have coincided with larger historical events. 68. Greenham. The Miners' strike. Events that at the time were simply part of the daily flow, but looking back seem pivotal, the colouring of an age.

Smash the Pigs. Smash the Pigs.

I try to remember what it felt like to be part of that crowd, to feel more connected to these events in my recent past than I do to the photographs of my parents taken before I was even born. But I can't. I know I was there. There I am standing in my tie-and-dye T-shirt, long hair down below my waist, next to a white sheet on which someone has dabbed *Say No to American Imperialism* in dripped black paint. But it seems like a thousand years ago. All those young people taking to the streets in a burst of idealism, unaware that they were projecting their frustration, their anger with their insurance salesman fathers, their spit-and-polish mothers onto the young Americans snatched from baseball games in Minneapolis and

98

backyards in Dakota, to fight a war in some part of the globe that the day before they hadn't even known existed.

I hadn't known what to expect, had just wanted the chance to take pictures. Being on my own, the camera justified me. I had so little chance to use it. "Art school, Hannah," my mother had insisted "is out of the question. Look at the type of girls who go there. All they do is wear black jumpers and hang around smoking. Typing. That's the thing to do, then you can get a proper job." My parents would have killed me if they'd known I was there at all, let alone on my own.

I'd never sensed danger before. Had anything to do with the police. Once the local constable had come to see my father after his new Rover had been broken into. He'd called him 'Sir' and sat under the hunting prints propped on the edge of the velvet Chesterfield in the drawing room by the coal fire with a cup of tea. Now they were all around on horses, armed with truncheons and visors and I was simply another teenager, in a shiny black PVC mac, among the hordes in headbands and smelly Afghan coats defiantly puffing on the occasional joint. But it had begun to work its way under my skin. The charred landscape and bombed paddy fields. The screaming children and bird-like women comatose among the smoking remains of bamboo huts flickering nightly in the corner of my room like grey ghosts. As the crowd surged down Oxford Street, past John Lewis, messages were barked through megaphones by official stewards. Some of the police wore riot gear, helmets that made them look like underwater divers. Cut off from the main body of the march a section was pushed into Derring Street where the top of the road had been blocked off. Unable to get back to join the others, demonstrators had gathered in the doorways of an Italian snackbar with mugs of dark tea and Mars bars.

"God I'm sorry. I've got a tissue somewhere," he offered plunging nervously into the various jacket pockets of his duffel coat, as the hot chocolate he'd spilled when he'd bumped into me scalded my fingers against the thin plastic cup. "Have I burnt you? Bloody careless of me," he said dabbing the front of my mac with a grubby tissue. "Name's Tom, by the way".

This is the first adult photograph I have of him. He is small and dark, and doesn't seem entirely at home in his body, as though he's somehow surprised that his mind should inhabit such an alien place, as if all those years when his emotions had to be locked away in the musty spare rooms of maiden aunts, buried in those cold school dormitories, had taken their toll. It's strange now seeing him with so much hair, almost down to his shoulders. He's wearing a corduroy jacket (he went on wearing it for years), his college scarf. Round wire glasses. He looks so young. Last time I caught a glimpse of him with the children he seemed to have aged. Bitterness doesn't suit him.

As the march moved off towards the American Embassy he kept dropping back to see that I hadn't been crushed by the crowd. Less flamboyant than his friends, he was reticent about asking me to join them in the pub after the march broke up. I'd never done anything like that before. Gone off with strangers. They'd come down that morning, he said. Skipped a tutorial and hitched down the A40. Decided it was more important than getting back an essay on Keynesian economics. The day before he had taken all his possessions – records, clarinet and books – to the Oxfam shop. The personal, he told me, was also the political.

"The problem, you see, with western society is we're defined by what we own, so that we, in turn, are defined by the material. Don't you agree?" he'd asked earnestly, "And you, tell me about you."

After that there were weekends in Oxford. Toast on the bars of the electric fire as rain pebbled the window of his freezing college room. Cheap incense and Bob Dylan's edgy wail trailing like sand-paper across cat gut. "You're my own sad-eyed lady of the lowlands," he'd joke, lying, on the floor, eyes closed, arms folded behind his head, in a thick cable-stitch sweater his mother had knitted for him. "Why d'you always look so sad?"

Some weekends he came down to London. We would get up late and have bangers and mash swimming in thick brown gravy in Henneky's on the corner of Westbourne Grove or spend all day in Portobello Road, trying on ratty fur coats, saffron-printed Indian dresses and cheese-cloth shirts. One day he found a leather bound copy of *Principia Mathematica* for 1s.

We bought cheap vegetables. Softening tomatoes, the last bruised mushrooms, a bottle of Algerian wine. I peeled the papery skin off fat cloves of garlic on the draining board of the landing sink, chopped onions, frying the hoops in a smear of green olive oil until transparent, adding the rice, wine and mushrooms to save on the washing up. I liked playing house. Perhaps Tom did too after all those school holidays spent in the clock-ticking mahogany drawing rooms of spinster aunts. In bed he'd teach me things, things I didn't know. About Keynes and Marx. He slept with his arm around me avoiding bits of my body as if they might overwhelm him. He made love quickly, ashamed by the necessity, by his inability to resist desire.

Sunday morning. Oxford. A sandstone city bathed in rose light. I was eighteen. We walked out to its edge, beyond the gargoyled spires, through the fields, across Christ Church meadows where the mist hovered above the damp marsh grass and he took my hand and swore – it makes me smile that I was so gullible – undying love. We both wanted, needed, each for our own reasons, to believe in that. Later we drank tea from thick mugs in the market café, the smoky sawdusted room crammed with cloth-capped traders and butchers in white aprons smeared with streaks of blood. Groups of students tucked into fried eggs and chips swimming in pools of grease. He bought me a bunch of violets, the sage leaves glistening with water. We wandered through the city as it was getting up, me carrying my flowers like a postulant, as students cycled lazily down Saint Aldgates, Sunday papers stuffed under their arms, out through its parks and gardens, to the river, where we punted up to the Vicky Arms and moored under the weeping willows and drank warm beer as the ducks uptailed in the murky water. And I thought, so this is it. This is love. I didn't realise it required anything of me. That I had choice.

"How could you? Couldn't you have had a bit more sense? What do you imagine people are saying behind your back? You never think do you Hannah?" My parents were furious when I became pregnant with Josh. By the time I'd faced up to it, it was already too late for an abortion. For weeks they wouldn't speak to me. Then one day they simply turned up on the doorstep of my digs, my father uncomfortable and incongruous among my Joan Baez posters and batiked banners, in his tweed sports jacket and club tie, my mother in her Jaeger camel. They sat awkwardly on the corner of the bed letting the tea I'd made them grow cold on the mantelpiece among the joss-sticks and Indian bells. I had no cups and saucers and they couldn't get used to the heavy pottery mugs. They had decided, they told me, my mother speaking for them both, that despite the fact that he seemed to have no idea what he was going to do with his future, and was, by their lights, immature, impractical and had little chance of earning a decent living, there was no alternative but for me to marry Tom. They would speak to his parents who still – it was, after all, all very well for them – knew nothing of the situation, swanning around as they were in Kenya. Now it had been decided, the sooner we got on with it the better.

So at the end of the summer term I gave up the job I'd only been doing for three months as secretary in a law firm and a striped marquee was set up on the lawn of my parents' house in Claygate and guests were invited. Jackie and I had made peace enough for her to be bridesmaid. We were married in church. "Hannah, we have to do it properly. My parents expect it," Tom said. For a while my father threatened not to come. He couldn't bear it. My Grandma Millie sniffed "Never been in a church and don't intend to now. Ridiculous a Jewish girl getting married in church," and stayed away. My other grandparents were dead so what they might have thought didn't matter. It was, in the end, a balmy July day. Mr. Wicks had mown the grass into bowling green stripes, and the pink buds of the rambling Albertina filled the garden with their heady scent. I wore an Empire-line dress and apple blossom in my hair. My father made a speech. We drank champagne and had our pictures taken in the rose garden by the fish pond, where once I had tried to kill Jackie.

✳

Aldgate, Aldersgate, Billingsgate, Bishopsgate, Cripplegate, Ludgate, Moorgate, Newgate. I extend my reach of London from the edges of the East End, where those who had been banished from the City crowded outside the ancient financial centre in rank rookeries, and walk along the remains of the Roman wall following its broken route. At Tower Hill, a cluster of Japanese tourists gathers to take a picture on the newly painted bridge as the river curls beneath them, a grey snake, its silver scales glistening in the morning sun. I walk up King William Street towards the Bank of England and the Mansion House. This is my father's domaine, the territory he had disappeared to each day on the train when I was a child. I don't feel comfortable here in this land of corporations and new money, among the young brokers from the floor of the Stock Exchange in their flamboyant braces and bright orange and green jackets looking like financial jockeys, as I walk past the chrome and glass Lloyds building, the Overseas Chinese Banking Corporation Ltd in Cannon Street. I can't take pictures here. I feel no connection to this powerhouse of faxes and mobile phones. I am happier in the market at Smithfield watching the porters lug huge sides of beef across their shoulders from the freezer lorries into the warehouses, or in the clutter of cheap china and bales of cut-price cloth of Petticoat Lane.

✳

Tom didn't, as I think he'd honestly expected he would, get the junior lectureship at St. Catherine's. Instead, after months of various applications around the country, he had taken the only job he was offered at Shepton Mallet College of Further Education. I didn't mind. I'd always wanted to live in the country.

The day we arrived in Somerset with our few belongings stuffed into a hired van, the lawn was a cloud of blue. It was April. Tiny stars of speedwell dotted the unmown grass, the scent of lilac filled the walled garden and beyond the high stone wall, in the crook of the valley, drummed the waterfall.

I went from room to room flinging open windows, letting sunlight into the musty corners, ripping up old linoleum to reveal huge granite flag-stones that had once been hauled up the steep hill by horse and cart from the local quarry. We scrubbed and painted, stripped the wood back to its natural grain, knocked down walls and unblocked ancient chimneys, and ate baked beans, faces smeared with soot and dust, by candlelight from the only two unpacked plates. And while Josh lay in his pram under the apple tree, I dug the garden and erected bean poles for scarlet runners and planted an espalier pear up the south facing wall. I bought six hens. Fat and brown like the drawings in Josh's picture book. *Sally Henny Penny will go barefoot, barefoot...* he'd shout, clapping podgy hands and toddling after them as soon as he could walk.

104

As we unloaded tea chests a young man with a wispy beard and baggy overwashed sweater wandered into the kitchen. Behind him, her doleful sheep's face framed by wispy hair, stood a blond woman and two grubby children with bare feet.

"Came to see who it was. Who'd moved in. Live at the bottom of the valley, end cottage. Make pots. Name's Peter," he said without introducing the others.

I offered them tea, which, despite his educated voice, he lapped, rather surprisingly, like a cat from the saucer. The two children drank nothing but hung onto their mother's long flowered skirt, its hem heavy with mud dripping over the tops of her wellingtons. She didn't speak, just peered out from behind the two curtains of drab dun hair. They simply stood in the corner of the kitchen staring and watching us unpack, then went. A few days later Peter left a bunch of carrots tied up by their green feathery leaves and an unplucked pigeon on our door step.

Slowly the days found their own rhythm. Pegging wet washing between the lilac trees, making bread from the coarse flour bought in sacks from the mill, reading to Josh by the ancient Aga on wet afternoons as the rain drip-dripped in the tall beeches. Sometimes we drove into Shepton Mallet to the rectory ground behind the church and I'd sit and watch him scamper like a monkey up the climbing frame and down the high slide. There was never anyone to talk to. Groups of local girls sat along the park wall gossiping, sharing bags of chips, their bare thighs bulging like fat chipolatas beneath tight mini-skirts, as a couple of farm lads sat in their black leathers revving parked motor bikes trying to impress them.

Tom was home less and less. He seemed to prefer the Common Room to the bottling and fermenting, the wet nappies and spilled Lego. It was as if the thin membrane of domestic intimacy was too much for him. He liked playing with Josh, building Lego towers and castles on the floor, but I needed him to cross the boundary of skin between us, to enter my head. I wanted him to do what he'd so rashly promised that day he had given me violets in Oxford; make me happy.

It was not all his fault. Sometimes I think I must have been born sad. God knows where it came from this blackness that seems to gather like clouds above the valley out of nowhere. Maybe I inherited it from my ancestors who brought it with them, like a roll of shot silk or a silver *menorah* out over the foothills, across the borders of Lithuania. My heritage in their exile. I couldn't escape it even as a child, lying in the long grass in the orchard at the bottom of the garden on a summer's afternoon, the sun on my back, as Jackie played doll's tea parties on the lawn. I'd lie hidden, watching a line of red ants roll their translucent eggs through the tall stems, threading yellow-faced daisies into rings and bracelets. Or later, when my mother, exasperated, told me 'to buck myself up' and go to the tennis club, where pink-scrubbed girls all curls and neat white pleats, flirted and joked with boys in V-necked cricket jumpers and sun-burnt arms, I simply couldn't shake it off. It accompanied me everywhere. A nanny, a fussy old chaperone who wouldn't let me out of her sight.

"Is it really worth all the effort?" Tom would ask with a sigh, looking up from his marking, as I came home from the corn merchant, the car laden with poles and chicken wire, for him to make a pen. "I haven't really got time. I've got to get on with my research, on top of all this," he nodded to the pile of unmarked essays. "You don't seem to understand, Hannah, how much time it takes. Shepton library is useless. I need specialist books. I'll have to go to Bath or Bristol. You don't know how difficult it is to do serious academic work without a university library."

So as he retreated into his books I baked and bottled fruit and dug my garden as if our survival depended on it, as if by offering up a constant stream of warm loaves and fresh brown eggs I could

106

somehow weld the whole shaky edifice together. He couldn't see I was trying to weave a web so intricate, so complex, it couldn't be unpicked.

More and more I spent time in the garden. I dug the vegetable patch, neglected for years, up by the stable, turning the crumbling clods, lining trenches with wet newspapers and steaming dung. I planned a crop rotation. Broad beans followed by wide leafed courgettes. My nails became black with ingrained crescents of earth. I hunted the library shelves for photographs of old gardens. Sissinghurst of the Sackville-Wests, Charleston, Thomas Hardy's cottage garden at Higher Bockhampton, scented with sweet peas, tall hollyhocks and lupines, colour stitched against the green like a Victorian sampler. Somewhere I found a copy of *An Account of a Cottage and Garden* published by *The Society for Bettering the Condition and Increasing the Comfort of the Poor.* The frontispiece showed lines of vegetables running in neat rows up to the walls of the low thatched dwelling.

I read books on foreign gardens. On the construction of Versailles, on the Alhambra of Granada, where the Emirs of Cordoba and Muslim lords created, behind fretworked shutters, behind masked doors and damask hangings, stained glass windows and *jalousies*, gardens of jasmine-scented shade and clear cool pools. Claustrophobic, strange, erotic.

I banned gaudy red geraniums, suburban lobelia and clumps of white alyssum. I wanted, behind my high stone walls, to recreate an authentic English garden. Subtle, understated and slightly scented; the blooms of the old Magenta rose and *La Reine Victoria* glorious only for a few fleeting days each summer. Their fragile petals destroyed by a sudden shower of rain, a too vigorous gust of wind. Banks of soft misty colour. Grey pinks fading into soft blues. I weeded the neglected herbaceous borders, dug out the white tendrils of bindweed with the prong of a fork. I planted catmint, dianthus, bronze fennel and verbascum. Lavender and buddleia for the butterflies. Around the kitchen door sowed aquilegia and placed flowerpots of marjoram and thyme and grey, woolly leafed sage, which I picked and dried. It felt as if I was not only doing battle for my life, but waging war on the surrounding fields and woods, constantly holding them off from encroaching on my newly dug beds. Often at sunrise I would be out in the garden while Tom and Josh still slept. The mornings smelt of damp grass and dew. I was at my happiest hoeing and watering, as the sun came up over the brow of the hill and the thrush broke into song in the far lilac.

The village didn't quite know what to make of us. We were the first incomers for years. They didn't know where to place us on the social scale of things, where we belonged. Dr. Russell they had always known. Retired now, he had trudged for thirty years through mud and slurry, thick drifts of snow with his small bag for the births of most of those over twenty and any of the deathbeds he could reach in time. Now everything was by appointment at the Health Centre and you never knew which doctor you'd get. Then there was the biographer Eustace Harwood. Tom had thought we might get invited for sherry. He'd had visions of being included at literary dinners, erudite conversations at the long oak dinner table with famous names down from London for the weekend. Pheasant and white bread sauce. The Harwoods had bought the house – squat Victorian Rococo – from the Dunmores in the late 40s, just after the war. A rural refuge for London literati tired of Spam and rationing. Auberon Waugh, Anthony Powell, C.P. Snow. An escape from tinned sardines in Lyons Corner House. Fresh eggs. Real butter. Bacon. We did get invited for sherry once. But it was made clear, after about three quarters of an hour, that our time was up. We were guided from the drawing room, with its high crammed bookcases and faded ormolu mirrors, chipped rosewood bureau and foxed water-colours, into the hall. Among the walking sticks and wax jackets, the cracked leather riding boots and dog baskets, Eustace Harwood shook hands in a manner that implied that he and his other guests were about to have lunch. We weren't asked again.

There wasn't a Post Office in the village. Stamps had to be bought at the top of the lane by banging on Arthur's kitchen door. Arthur ran the farm and his wife was the sub-postmistress. In the corner of her kitchen was a set of brass scales, for weighing packages, beside a fat leather book full of different denomination stamps. But she never opened at regular hours. It was supposed to be between nine-thirty and twelve. But on market days and days she simply didn't feel like it, she wouldn't be in. Sometimes you'd have to go across to the pub to find out where she was.

I'd heard rumours about the pub's landlord. The pub belonged to his mother but she stayed in bed all day upstairs, was too fat to get up and had varicose veins like knots of blue string. It was said she made him live in the caravan at the back with his dog and take his meals outside. Although he must have been about forty she wouldn't let him get married. Not that any one in their right mind would have had him. I'd been told he had no front teeth and kept a shot gun under the counter. Both were true. At one end by the fire, the same two old men always played shove halfpenny. At the other was a broken table, an old bedstead and pair of broken rusty bikes. The floor was covered with sawdust darkened by puddles of beer.

For weeks Tom left on his bike first thing in the morning and came home about seven. He seemed to stay at college for every meeting. Then when he got home he'd shut himself in the spare room with piles of marking. My days consisted of cooking and gardening with Josh, feeding the hens. Tom only existed on the margins. I hardly spoke to another adult. One afternoon I walked with Josh down to Peter's cottage. The blond woman, Sky she called herself, was there with the children but he was out. She nodded silently as we hovered at the kitchen door. The table was a jumble of half-drunk mugs of cold tea, old letters, scribbled colouring books and jars of lidless crystallised marmalade. A black frying pan lay in the middle, the fat congealed around two squiggles of burnt bacon. Socks, children's pants and shoes were strewn across the floor and the sagging armchair covered with dog hairs. In a toy box, Josh found a yellow wheelless truck which he began to push across the floor. But Sky's son grabbed it, thumping him hard in the chest, shoving it possessively back in the box. Sky moved slowly towards him as if about to remonstrate but then said nothing. Offended, Josh climbed onto my knee, curled up and began to suck his thumb.

As I drank the dark over-brewed tea from a cracked cup, I tried to start a conversation. It would've been good to have a friendly neighbour. But Sky answered in monosyllables as she busied herself unravelling tangled balls of wool beside a vast loom that took up all the space under the stairs. It seemed to make no difference to her whether I was there or not. I finished my tea and left.

There are so many photos of Josh. A few hours old, wrapped in a shawl Tom's mother crocheted for him. Asleep in his crib. Crawling on the lawn. But this is one of the ones I love best. Late summer. Josh with corn-blond hair in big dungarees in the middle of a field of long grass. I took a lot of photos of him that summer. It's painful to see him so free, so untouched by experience, and to think of him now. Angular, angry, hurt.

June. The field was an explosion of ox-lips, moon daisies and wild orchids, the lane filled with cow parsley, sky-blue sorrel and ragged robin. We picked armfuls, filling jam jars in every room of the house. I couldn't get used to the excess. The photographs I took look like Dutch flower paintings. The light flooding from behind.

It was an old meadow, undisturbed by cultivation. Only a few cows grazed lazily down by the stream wading into the squelching mud to drink in the shade of the overhanging hawthorns, their rope tails swishing at flies, their dusty coats steaming. In one hand I carried a basket, in the other Josh's sticky fingers lay curled in my palm, as he trailed beside me, slow and pregnant, his face streaked with purple juice.

In and out our fingers moved, between the sharp thorns, searching out the firm black cushions which hadn't begun to ferment, as we left the soft, overripe berries to the wasps. Josh carried a little earthenware bowl. But it remained empty as he ate everything he picked. Beyond the sound of the wasps and the waterfall, a distant tractor grumbled somewhere over the hill.

No one came here, except Peter. I don't know what had happened to him in the months after he'd first come into our kitchen. I knew there'd been terrible rows and that he no longer lived in the cottage with the blond woman and the children. His hair had become wild and matted, his nails frayed black. He seemed to have moved into some sort of hut in the middle of the wood. Illegal electricity cables looped like Christmas decorations off the main telegraph wires. The first time I saw him talking to himself, laying snares for rabbits, I snatched up Josh, terrified, and ran back to the cottage. After that I often saw him out with his gun shooting magpies. I never knew why he lived in the wood, what had happened. I thought of my Aunt Dot. I'd never known her but she inhabited the edges of my childhood like a grey ghost. Something had happened to her as well. Something secret that meant that she'd been locked away down the end of a long green corridor wearing somebody else's boiled woollen cardigan and faded dress. Rolled stockings round her ankles. Something to do with a married man, an inappropriate love. Occasionally Peter would simply appear in my kitchen unannounced. He would sit in silence while I chopped windfalls for chutney, sipping tea from a saucer, as I worked among the smells of vinegar, cinnamon and nutmeg, scalding jam jars, adding little wax discs and labels in clear black ink. Green tomato. Apple and raisin.

In the Autumn he left shaggy ink caps and puff balls on my doorstep, bloated and white as an old man's belly.

It was Peter who showed me the chimneys. Deep in the wood by the stream. Huge ivy covered stacks and a rusting iron sluice that divided the stream just below a pair of deserted cottages. Once it had been a bustling iron works making edge tools. Scythes, ploughshares, coulters, for farmers as far away as Exeter. That was before the Birmingham industry, with its new-fangled machines, destroyed the trade. The Dunmores, once local yeomen, had built the dumpy Rococo house on the hill and the ornate neo-Gothic church as a living for their youngest son, from the proceeds. Now spongy lichen and ferns sprouted in dank culverts, clung to the dripping stones.

After we'd filled two plastic bags with fruit, we stretched out in the long grass. It was still hot for September. Our limbs relaxed in the warmth. Full and fed up with picking, Josh lay beside me in the shade of the blackberry bush, his small head nuzzled in the crook of my arm, while he sleepily arranged flowers on my distended belly as we drifted in and out of sleep beneath the high note of a sky lark. Hidden in our nest of grass, the earth warm against our backs, I didn't see the dark shadows lurking deep in the pine trees behind the cottage.

✳

When I get back from Greece there's a note from Della pinned on my front door.

Took in a registered letter for you while you were away. Will bring up when back – D.

"Saw your light on Han, so guessed you was back," she says. It's late, she's all dressed up on her way to the club. "Cor! You're brown! Here's the letter. Had to sign for it. Hope it's not the law after you. But you don't look like the sort to rob a bank! Look must dash or Dave'll have me guts for garters if I'm late. Tell me all about it. Hope you had a good time."

It's another affidavit. This time from Alison. It says that without responsible discussion I'd abandoned the children in order to go off to Greece. That if it had not been for her and Tom they might well have been left on their own. It says that when the children arrived to stay with them Josh was in rags and Annie had nits. That these are obvious signs of my neglect and my inability to cope. I've never ever left the children alone. Doesn't she realise that Josh cut that hole in the knee of his jeans and frayed·the edges deliberately? I was furious too, I'd just bought them. As to the damn nits. The whole school is plagued with them. Annie screams at me every time I go near her with that metal comb and noxious lotion. Oh God. I feel as though they are closing in.

✳

I'm anxious, too, about the exhibition. I have to work. I am losing the thread. I feel too distracted by what's going on with Tom. But I have to keep going. It was all very well winning the competition, but now I have to produce a body of work. When my head is clear I see photographs everywhere, they come from the world to me, without my asking. I know now that it's the small losses of the East End I want to photograph. Both architectural and human. The histories that have been obliterated by time and ill luck. I want to reveal them, to strip back the layers. It's not shock I am after but the unmasking of something hidden, tender, of which the subject is unaware.

✳

"I'll be very discreet. If you can just give me a few hours to wander round with my camera, have a brief chat."

Booth House. 195 Whitechapel Road. Home of The Salvation Army. Just east past the Whitechapel Art Gallery and library. I turn out of the tube. On the opposite side of the road, the roof of the mosque shines gold in the pale sunlight. I'm nervous. Don't know what to expect. I came here to look for my Jewish roots, thinking somehow that would define me but I seem to have ended up with the dispossessed. I have visions of Orwell queuing for a bed in a spike among the lousy and the homeless, the alcoholic and abusive. But the building looks like a provincial polytechnic. The hall all polished linoleum and dusty rubber plants. It was built in the late 60s as a working men's hostel for those fleeing from unemployment in Glasgow, the North East or Derry, to work for cash hodding bricks or mixing cement on London construction sites. I was told, when I rang, to ask for the duty officer. I stick my head through an open glass partition into a small office. "Yes, that's me, Eileen," says a young women with aggressively cropped hair and a sweet smile. She wears black jeans and a man's shirt buttoned at the neck. A forest of keys dangles from her belt. I follow her down the relentlessly cheerful passage, with its bright yellow curtains and reproduction of *The Laughing Cavalier* in a gilt plastic frame. An elderly woman in a purple nylon overall is mopping an already spotless floor. In the empty dining room, net curtains hang at the window in an approximation of suburban domesticity. Each red formica table has a vase of plastic flowers. I'd expected dormitories, men rowed side by side in bunks under grey Salvation Army blankets, unable to sleep for the rantings of other inmates. Instead there are single rooms. Narrow bed, sink, side board and cupboard. "Oh that's all over. There's hardly any hostels like that any more. Only at Christmas when *Crisis* sets up soup kitchens," Eileen says quietly closing the door of the room she's just shown me.

Haili Salasi. Another time he was found striding up and down a smoking balcony baying at the moon, having burnt his top-floor flat to a blackened shell. His huge head fills the picture frame with its froth of hair like a halo of white tongues. A black Moses or Marx.

Some of the men, I learn, used to be dockers. Theirs was a tradition of heavy drinking. Waterside workers were hired and paid in pubs, sometimes they set up bars in the holds of the ships with filched grog. The dockside pubs, like the local market bars in Smithfield and Billingsgate, had special licences to serve alcohol in the morning. At one time, an old navvy who was born just off Brick Lane tells me, one Bethnal Green cross road boasted three pubs on its four corners. When the jobs went, the drinking habit remained. Scraggy used to live in Limehouse. "Behind the Chinese laundry", he tells me, coming over to see what I'm doing as I re-load the camera. "Washing either smelt of boiled noodles or the noodles of boiled bloody washing. Can't remember which." He'd worked in the East India Docks. "Ships came from all over. Russia. Argentina. Fruit, steel, coal. You name it, we unloaded it." His huge meat-cleaver hands are a delta of blue scars. His face is puffy with fluid retention and liver failure. The once bright eyes, now dirty and dimmed. "First they brought in them containers. Now with Thatcher the 'ole lot is finished. We was all laid off. Me Mrs passed away just before they knocked down the flats last year. Glycoma. All sold off for the Limehouse Link, wasn't it. Right over our heads. Never asked us did they?" he continues in a series of rhetorical questions addressed as much to himself as to me. "All to get some bleeding journalists to work (if you'll pardon the language). Couldn't settle after that. Different if I'd still had me boy. But I was away see," his voice becomes barely audible, "in the army. Gibraltar. He were ten. Burst appendix. Never saw him again did I? So then it was Special Brew and Tenants Super for breakfast. Best pain relief in the world. But you can't keep on. They saved me," he

116

nods in the general direction of the office. " Can't stay 'ere if you're pissed see. Had the DTs one night in the church yard. Them skin heads came and done me in. Kicked me flaming teeth out with them big bloody boots. Mangled bloody mess. Look 'ere," he says fishing in his mouth, pulling out a set of top dentures to show me his bald pink gums.

At first he's wary when I ask him if I can take his picture. But after he agrees he is extremely co-operative, full of ideas about where he should stand, and suggestions for interesting backgrounds. Before the drink, he must have had a real intelligence. After Scraggy I wander round and take another couple of rolls; of Mickey the old ganger from Co. Clare with a face like a squashed prune, of Dino with the broken nose and a dotted necklace of blue around his throat that says *Cut Here*. When I knock on the office door Captain Edwards gets up and warmly shakes my hand, blushing a little as he does so. His Salvation Army tie rests on a gently rounded belly. He wears wire rimmed glasses. A close cropped beard covers an affable double chin. "Come in, come in Hannah. Seen all you want? Eileen shown you everything? This, by the way, is my wife" he says smiling across at a small dark woman in a crisp white shirt with epaulettes, filing papers behind the desk. "Cup of tea?"

I park myself beside the filing cabinet with the mug.

"So what's this for then Hannah, if you don't mind me asking?"

"An exhibition. At the Whitechapel. I won a photographic competition and they've offered me an exhibition. I'm interested in the East End. I suppose it's a sort of voyage of self-discovery. My family came from round her. Though it was a long time ago. I'm Jewish".

"Not many of them left. Mostly Bengalis now as you can see. Changes all the time the East End. Nature of the place. The Army's been working here for years. You've heard of The Temperance Movement? That's how it all started. The East End's always attracted those with problems. The ones who don't belong or feel comfortable anywhere else. They just sort of gravitate here. Some make a go of it. Others just sink. Well," he continues cheerily "when will we be able to see this exhibition then, Hannah? You'll send us an invitation I hope," he says after I take his portrait in full uniform in the hall. "If you need to come back, just give us a ring anytime," he says extending his hand warmly as he shows me out. "Nice to have met you."

The sun has come out. It's lunchtime. A group of Asian school girls in silk trousers and stilettos clatters down the street arm in arm, gossiping and drinking cans of coke. Their dark hair is curled into pony tails held by diamonte clips. All wear dangly gold earrings, have eyes rimmed with kohl. I turn down Brick Lane in search of a samosa and walk up past the glass-fronted Truman's brewery with its smudged reflection of the old side of the street, past Atlantis, the huge artists' warehouse where you can buy anything from linseed and turps, tubes of oil or sheets of gold leaf, charcoal and graphite sticks, to calligraphy pens and handmade papers from India and Japan. I cross over the road and walk down Fournier Street towards the Hawksmoor church.

"'Ello darling."

It's Mary. I'd hoped to see her. It gives me pleasure that over the past months since she first spat at me and told me to frig off, she seems to have come to consider me as a friend. She's Irish. Sixty? Seventy? Forty? Who knows? Seven children. One dead. Two in Australia. The others in Dublin or missing. As usual she carries two stuffed *Safeway* carrier bags, wears three great coats and a pair of army boots. At first I was scared. Put off by the dirt and the smell, her agressive attitude. But *she* befriended *me* when she saw me taking photos and now I'm pleased to see her.

"You'll be wanting me picture then Hannah?" she offers in her still soft brogue, that carries in its depths, wet emerald fields, the musk of a cow's flank at milking. Her face cracks into a grubby smile as she flirtatiously pulls her coats up over her swollen mottled knees offering me a mock glamour pose. Jutting hip. Pouting lips revealing stumps of blackened teeth.

"Sure 'tis me one chance of fame. Oie 'spect to be having me photo soon in that big gallery. I'm waiting on you making me famous darlin'?"

"We'll see what we can do for you Mary," I say focusing my camera, taking advantage of her playful mood, as I run off a roll of film.

I've never learnt exactly where she came from. She offers me snippets. Rural Ireland, a violent father, a drunken husband. Something I can never quite piece together about her dead child. Her face is a chart calibrating the degrees of abuse and pain she's endured. She poses for me as long as I need, smiling her beautiful black toothed smile.

"Marilyn Monroe couldn't have done better herself. Enjoy your tea and buy a cake," I say slipping a couple of quid into her leathery palm.

✳

Christmas Eve. The photos of the last Christmas we spent at the cottage. Josh has hung his Christmas stocking with a scrawled note on the beam above the fire. The letters are all different sizes. The *F* of father enormous, the *CH* of Christmas tiny and run together. I remember him writing it. He took hours sitting at the table with his felt tips, his tongue poking from the corner of his lips in concentration.

I turned over and tried to go back to sleep ignoring the contractions clawing my abdomen, the gnawing steel teeth at the small of my back. It was too soon, the wrong day. I was too tired. The baby wasn't due for another three weeks. I crept out of bed into the silent house leaving Tom sleeping. The flag-stones in the kitchen were icy against my feet. Clasping the rail of the Aga I nuzzled into its iron warmth, as the pain blossomed outward like a Japanese paper flower opening in water. In the corner the lights of the tree twinkled in the dark and I was flooded by the same unnameable longing I'd felt as a child, standing in my flower-sprigged nightie in front of the Christmas tree, by those heavy velvet curtains, in my parents' dining room.

Trailed across the dresser, behind the rows of mugs, the pots of last summer's strawberry jam, were loops of ivy Josh and I had pulled off the garden wall that morning. In the middle was a cotton-wool snowman he'd made from a toilet roll at playschool. A large jug of holly sprayed and smothered in mounds of gluey glitter stood on the sill. In the dark my bare feet shimmered with the golden spangles he had scattered across the floor. That morning we'd gone into town. It was market day, the stalls full of holly wreaths, mistletoe and flame-leafed poinsettias. Rows of plucked turkeys and limp hares, their long ears spotted with blood, hung suspended from iron hooks. Josh had stood transfixed by the turkeys' dangling broken necks, their clawed feet and beady eyes. Outside The George, the Salvation Army band played carols, rattled collection boxes as families hurried across the square carrying shopping and Christmas trees. Across the new precinct floated the tannoyed strains of *I'm Dreaming of a White Christmas*.

Despite the warmth of the Aga, I was shivering. All day I'd been filling mince pies, making patés, wrapping presents in bright tissue for Josh's stocking. Fat wax crayons, chocolate money, a bag of marbles like the ones I'd hidden from Jackie in the attic as a child. Now the pains were coming every five minutes. Then just after midnight it came, the gush of wetness. I went and woke Tom. "Are you sure? It's too early isn't it?" he said pulling the duvet up round his ears and rolling over.

120

The coldest night of the year. The road black glass under the headlights as we drove the top way over the fields to the hospital. Newly ploughed furrows sparkled in metallic waves under pin-hole stars. Deep in the winter wheat rabbits lay hidden, flattened against the frozen earth, their ears pricked to the wind, as Josh curled dreaming under his duvet of Father Christmas, and my father lay, open mouthed, on his back, snoring in the spare room, in the twin bed next to my mother.

"A bed pan. I think I need a bed pan," I murmured too late, shit running down my legs. Ashamed, no longer sure he loved me enough to see me like this.

"Good girl. Come on, some nice shallow breaths now. That's it. Count. That's it. G-o—o-d. Still be a little while yet, you're not fully dilated. I'll be back in about ten minutes to see how you're doing."

I didn't want the nurse to leave but didn't want to make a fuss. I wanted to be good, to do this properly. I wanted to please. Just as I had in that cold morning room trying to learn those arpeggios my dyslexic fingers couldn't accommodate for my father, or when a spotty faced boy in a curtain of overcoats had once got me to jerk him off, leaving a damp patch down the front of my new blue dance dress. The room was white and silent except for the hum of the electric clock and the sound of my own dog-like panting. On a trolley lay a row of gleaming instruments. Scalpel, forceps, speculum. It was three in the morning and the hospital seemed empty. It was already Christmas day. I'd forgotten how bad the pain was. Blanked it out. Nature's sneaky trick to make you forget until the next time. The contractions crashed like breakers on shingle until I thought I would split from end to end. I grabbed the black rubber mask gulping in mouthfuls of gas and air until my head swam and I felt sick.

Suddenly I was very cold.

"Remind me why I'm doing this, help me," I sobbed turning to

Tom remembering those nights when he'd lain stiffly by my side, the climbing rose tapping in the wind against the window, trying to talk him into another baby. "A family Tom. You don't want Joshy to grow up alone, an only child." And then one night, after I'd been taking my temperature to gauge the best time, even though we had not made love for months, he'd turned to me, taken my hand and placed it around his swollen prick, then without so much as a kiss, had straddled me, holding my shoulders and thrusting with a quick, quiet desperation till he came with a small shudder. Now he said nothing, as above the white mask his eyes darkened, at my doubt about the child I'd persuaded him to have.

"Come on now push. Good girl," encouraged the freckled nurse."Well done! Push th-a-t's it. Right down into your bottom."

"I can't, I can't do it any more. I can't fucking well do any of it any more," I screamed through gritted teeth, gulping another whiff from the rubber mask, my legs, under the sodium glare strung up in steel stirrups, like the trussed turkeys in the market.

"Of course you can, you're nearly there. Th-a-t's it. It's got a mop of dark hair, come on now, one more push."

With her slanted almond eyes, her black spiky hair she looked like a changeling. I'd never wanted a daughter. Saw myself as the mother of sons. Didn't feel confident enough to produce a replica of myself, trust myself to sense where I ended and she began. I was afraid of re-encountering the small girl who'd not been able to make sense of it all, who'd rummaged through yellowing tissue paper in the back of wardrobes, dug through her father's desk draws in search of secrets she couldn't even name. Yet there she was, my daughter, entirely herself. Beautiful.

"She's lovely isn't she? Aren't you a bit glad we've had a girl?" I asked cradling the downy head against my shoulder.

"Why ask me that?" and I saw, now that he'd removed the surgical mask, that Tom looked drained. And then I knew, with some

122

atavistic animal instinct, that he had already left. With Josh he'd wiped my cracked lips with a moist sponge, brushed back damp strands of hair from my forehead as I panted and puffed through the long night. For eight hours, like someone drowning, I'd clutched his hand until the blood stopped and his wedding ring left a deep indentation in his finger. But this time it had been different. She was his pay off. His guilt child.

✳

I've wondered so often about this capacity for self deceit that makes us deny what's happening under our very noses. I knew something had changed the day he came back from the conference at the LSE. The burst of enthusiasm, the edgy excitement.

"Hannah, it's fantastic. This woman Alison – she's a full time lecturer – wants me to co-write a book. Seems we're working in exactly the same areas. It's my chance to publish something really good, get a decent academic post." What could I say then as her letters dropped two three four times a week on my mat, letters from another woman, as threatening as a seductively plunging cleavage? This was serious research. I wouldn't understand.

✳

Quiet and clean in the dim dawn light and nothing but the sweet smell of her milky breath. Tom had gone to catch some sleep before Josh woke bouncing with excitement to open his Christmas stocking. Alone with Annie I unwrapped a tiny hand from the tight swaddling of pink airtex, uncurling the fine creased fingers. Her pearl-shell nails perfect, only miniature. How many women, amazed at their own handiwork that dark winter morning, were doing the same…one two three four five…

Her skin was mottled, almost transparent, as if unaccustomed to the light. Spiky down covered her head like the spines of a sea urchin. As she nuzzled my night-dress I felt a gush and unbuttoned it. The pain made me start. I could hear the milk dropping into her empty stomach as she gave little grunts and snorts between the sucks. Five in the morning. It felt as if we were the only people in the world. She lay in my arms looking straight at me. She looked so vulnerable. I was overwhelmed by her smallness, the fragile nape of her neck that might be snapped with one flick, the tiny blotchy frog feet. And then I realised I was sobbing.

"Hello," I whispered " Welcome to the world." And her eyes met mine, knowing, black, quizzical.

✳

A dusting of hoar frost melts in the watery sun, green buds erupt from dead wood. There is Annie, in a pram, under the apple tree watching the branches web the duck-egg sky as I heave a mound of wet nappies from the basket and peg them, a row of awning, between the lilac trees in the snapping wind. From the roof of the greenhouse a thrush is singing. In the left hand corner of the frame is the blur of Josh's thumb.

As Annie slept, Josh and I collected eggs from the hens and milked the goat. He'd learnt to squeeze and pull the fleshy udders so she didn't kick or pull away and the watery jets spurted straight into the chipped enamel jug. Later we made yoghurt, scalding raw milk in a shallow pan. Josh stood beside me on a wooden chair stirring in the culture. Carefully we'd pour the warm mixture into screw-top jars which we buried behind piles of drying clothes and steps of crisp sheets in the airing cupboard. The whole house seemed to be a process of fermentation. Mung beans sprouted in the dark, demijohns of damson and elder-flower wine bubbled in the larder, loaves of stone-ground bread rose on the Aga. Process versus stasis. And all the while Alison's letters kept on coming.

More and more our lives moved on parallel lines.

"Hannah I really do put my foot down at bees."

"Why? I might make some money if I can sell the honey. I could try the WI stall on market days."

"That's rubbish. It'll be like the hens. That cost thirty quid for the poles and the wire, let alone the chicken house and the feed. It'll be at least two years before you make a profit. And I simply haven't got time to help. Sometimes you really do try my patience. Be a bit more practical can't you? I have to have the first three chapters ready to send to Alison by the end of term. If you want bees as a hobby then that's fine, it's up to you, but I haven't got time to mess around."

But I ordered beegloves with massive gauntlets, a hat and veil and a bee-proof overall with elastic cuffs and ankles to prevent the bees climbing inside my clothes. I went to the local bee-keepers' meetings and brought the British Bee Keeper Association monthly journal and Bee Craft and placed hives under the lilac trees. Then I set up a brood chamber and waited for the first granulated combs.

The original chickens I'd bought were becoming old and scrawny. I didn't realise what vicious beasts they were, hadn't understood the full meaning of 'hen-pecked' until I saw them attacking one of the weaker birds. I should have killed them when they stopped laying, wrung their necks. But I couldn't. So I stopped eating meat. I strove for purity, became an aesthete in an attempt to control my crumbling world. I'd liked to have existed on carrots and beans.

✳

A crisp February morning. Mist low across the fields. The first catkins in woolly clusters burst from the hazels. Clumps of snow-

125

drops poke through iron ground under the apple tree, white petals tinged with a web of green veins.

"Here Hannah, you take Josh and the push chair. I'll carry Annie and the bag," Marion offered as we bundled onto the bus full of women with back packs, small children in South American hats and wellingtons. I'd recently met her and the other women I was going to Greenham with when I'd joined the Shepton Mallet *Women Against Greenham* group.

"Anyone want an oat flapjack?" a large woman in layers of striped hand-knitted jumpers called from the front of the coach. "Pass the box round," she instructed regally waving a copious Tupperware container.

Half a mile from the camp the bus dropped us off. We must have looked like a band of refugees. Women with bundles, babies and buggies straggled down the mud-splattered road towards the base. The air was thick with curried vegiburgers smoking on barbecues at makeshift roadside stalls. At each gate, tents had sprung up like Indian villages. Sleeping bags hung airing from guy ropes, snotty faced kids played in the mud as women collected wood, peeled potatoes. I'd brought my camera. It was my first public admission for a long time that I took photos. It was years since I'd taken to the streets with my camera and followed the march to Grosvenor Square. Since then there had only been the odd evening class. Still lives set up on the kitchen table when the kids were at school. My 'hobby' as Tom called it. Yet when I was in the makeshift dark-room under the stairs I felt a sort of calm I experienced nowhere else.

The perimeter fence had been decorated with motifs woven into the wire. Plaited grass and dried flowers. Babygrows and teddies splayed like tiny crucifixions in the mesh. Children's paintings and batiked doves. On the other side a young American marine, stood self-consciously at ease, holding a rifle.

We shall, we shall not be moved

We linked hands around the whole base. Children, grand-mothers, pregnant women. "Hannah it won't make one jot of differ-ence. A few women are hardly going to influence the whole US government strategy are they? You need to be organised. Popular uprisings need leaders. If you really care about disarmament, lobby your MP. A few spells and incantations by a bunch of New Age feminists aren't going to do much good." Perhaps he'd forgotten we had met in Grosvenor Square.

I'd been attending meetings for a few months. The squares of the calendar filling with appointments gave my life new meaning. Out of the blue, down the muddy track, a phalanx of mounted police appeared. Three abreast, the flanks of their bay horses steamed in the frosty air. Their truncheons nuzzled like black snouts beside their long polished boots. Suddenly a cry went up "The line is breaking. Hold on. Don't let them break the line", as mothers were parted from toddlers, babies began to cry and the human chain scattered in all directions.

Further down the fence there was a lot of shouting and commotion. Rumour and counter rumour buzzed through the crowd. Two women had got through. Sliced through the fence. No one really knew what had happened. We heard later, the woman in the striped jumper had been arrested. On the coach home the party atmosphere had evaporated as women sat in small cold groups quietly humming.

"Had a good time?" Tom asked, glancing up from his marking, as I staggered into the kitchen past midnight, tired and muddy, Josh hanging half asleep around my neck and Annie bundled up in her push chair.

✳

A winter of blue frost and icicles. The country was falling apart. The miners' strike, power cuts, rubbish in the streets, the three day week. We huddled by candle light around the wood fire as if under siege. For days it snowed. A tin sky. Drifts blew across the fields piling on the tops of hedges up to the telegraph wires. In the mornings we had to dig our way out of the front door. The worst winter for fifteen years. We couldn't get the car out. Had to leave it at the top of the lane. It took an hour and twenty minutes to drive into Shepton three miles away. Tom had to walk to work, sinking to the knees in drifts as he cut across the fields. He wouldn't take time off. He would rather be at college. He seemed trapped and restless at home. Outside the snow fell in large flat flakes turning the fields into a patchwork of white lint. The log pile, the chicken-house, the steaming dung heap outside the goat's stall disappeared under a bandage of snow. The only person who got through was the postman, so that Alison's letters continued to blow through my letter box like sheets of ice.

My days lost colour. It was so cold all the bees died. In bed at night we lay side by side, chill as stone effigies. Tom had never liked touch, felt constrained by his own physical needs.

Hours, days, slipped away. The skeins were falling through my fingers. I couldn't get out of bed. I simply let Tom take over the children, move into the space left by my shadow.

"Why is this place always such a Goddam mess," I yelled.

I dreaded him coming home. He went straight to the children's rooms to begin the next chapter of their bedtime story.

"Go on Dad. Read us the next bit of the BFG. Go on please. Be your best friend," bribed Josh.

"I'm not cooking your fucking dinner unless you come and eat it," I screamed up the stairs, unable to identify other meanings, other words.

"Hannah do try and get a grip on yourself. Your behaviour is hardly an example to the children," he said emerging ten minutes later sniffing at the words like a bad cooking smell and watching, with detached amusement, as I tipped a steaming pile of beans and carrots from the heavy iron pot onto the kitchen table.

"Satisfied?" he asked as I burst into tears.

Next day I went to the doctor, then tore up the prescription he gave me and threw it in the bin in the street. I had Annie with me and we wandered into town pushing her push-chair past the deconsecrated Methodist chapel where the couple from London stripped old pine in a tank of caustic acid in the aisle, past the Health Food shop, down to the cattle market. "Cows, moocows," Annie chortled as we watched the terrified calves being loaded into the back of a lorry, their spindly legs clamped in resistance against the ramp as farm hands grabbed them by their ears and tails to shove them on board.

The skirt was compensation. While Josh was at playschool I loaded Annie into the back of the car and went into Bath. I hated shopping but all my old clothes pulled across my stomach, strained the material at the button holes. Since I'd had Annie I lived in T-shirts and jeans. Everything I tried on seemed unsuitable for a feeding mother. In the end I bought a flowing patchwork skirt in different coloured silks. It was too dressy and too expensive but it fitted.

I knew the moment he came through the door and found me mopping squashed bananas and fish fingers from the kitchen floor in my new skirt he'd forgotten.

"But I reminded you this morning, on your way out," I snapped.

"Hannah what are you doing? Why are you cleaning the floor in that skirt? Is that what the smart young housewife is wearing to cook her children's supper nowadays?"

"I was just trying to get the kids fed and clear up a bit. I couldn't leave it for the baby sitter could I? And I had nothing to wear. I had to buy something."

"How much?"

"Fifty pounds."

"You wear a fifty pound skirt to mop the kitchen floor." I felt the tears starting to prick behind my eyelids. I blinked in an effort to hold them back, to prevent a scene.

"OK. OK," he said his tone softening. "So you bought a fifty pound skirt and you're cleaning the kitchen floor in it. So it's not the end of the world," he said putting his arm around me as he might Annie if she'd fallen and grazed her knee. And with that gesture my defences crumbled. I couldn't hold on anymore and let my head fall against his chest. "Tom, don't leave me. Please, please don't leave me."

The room was elegant. High Georgian windows covered by swagged peach drapes. A group of flower prints hung over the velvet Chesterfield. Dr. Bagley's wife had organised the evening to raise money for the playschool. Her daughter Sophie went there with Josh. On the marble mantelpiece, between the wedding photos and the portraits of two small children, brown and grinning in front of a sheet of sparkling blue sea, stood a silver rose bowl filled with peach roses.

"Darling," I could hear her saying as she leant a silk arm across her husband's cashmere shoulder, "I think we're going to need some more white wine." And across the room I watched Tom talking to one of the practice partners, watched the formal, jerky movements, the discomfort with his own body. He avoided me all evening.

Later in bed, while he took the baby-sitter home, I dozed and waited for the sound of the car's crunch outside. Floating in and out of sleep, I was back in my parents' house, dreaming of my mother's silk scarves, the lace-edged handkerchiefs smelling of Chanel No.5, the pots of rouge and little boxes of mascara she kept on her dressing table. Of attics crammed with wicker picnic hampers, tartan travelling rugs, hidden secrets.

In the moonlight, as the shadows from the rambling rose coiled like barbed wire across the ceiling, I tried to forget that I'd ever seen them. Blot out that Sainsbury's carrier bag I'd found in the attic, looking for the children's snow boots, full of letters in Alison's thin cramped hand: *Tom, my darling, it's too great a sacrifice. I admire your loyalty, your fortitude but is she really worth it? I am waiting for you... I love you A.*

At 1.30 I woke to find him undressing, dropping his clothes at the foot of the bed. He climbed in beside me and turned without speaking on his side, his back a familiar white arc in the half-light. I prised myself awake. I didn't want him to retreat into sleep. In the darkness I folded myself silently around his curved shape like a drowning swimmer clings piggy back to a life-saver. His body was tense, his arm rigid, forming a protective shield over his groin. Beneath the covers I moved my hand over his buttock and thigh but he pushed it away. And I realised in that second what was happening. That he felt as if he was being unfaithful. That I was now the other woman. That he could not touch me because to do so would be a betrayal of Alison. And in my fear, on the far, cold side of the bed to which I had been banished, I asked hesitatingly:

"Did you ring the Marriage Guidance people ?"

"No, I decided not to."

"Why? Why not. You said you would, you promised." I could hear my own voice pressing, urgent, already anticipating the reply, wanting it to be out in the open.

"Because there's no point. I'm leaving, Hannah. I'm going to live with Alison."

I could not speak, felt as though I'd never be able to cross the white tundra of silence between us.

"But what about the children?" I managed to ask, my voice a dry whisper.

"I want them. I mean it Hannah, if you try and keep them I'll fight you through the courts. I'll tell them all I know...."

✳

131

A row of white-washed cottages right on the tip of the headland. And nothing but gorse and rabbits' droppings between them and the endless blue of the sea. The photo shows tiny sheltered yards nestling behind high walls protected from the briny wind. Purple and crimson fuchsia grow wild. At the end of the point is a light-house. The polished brass chronometer and a vast concave lens glints like Cyclops's eye out across the flinty Atlantic. The house shakes each time the fog horn booms out through the heavy blanket of mist.

It had been Marion's suggestion. She'd rung suddenly out of the blue. The cottage belonged to her cousin, a mineralogist away on a field trip. He wanted someone to look after the place. "It's perfect for the children, Hannah. You can have it for the week over the Spring Bank holiday. It'll hardly cost you anything. Derek and I can't go because of his mother and Donald doesn't like leaving it empty over the holiday and wants someone there to keep an eye on the place."

Low ceilings and beams. There were two tiny bedrooms. The walls were two feet thick and above the fireplace on the white-washed wall were maps and charts of the tide-times and a framed case of nautical knots. In the cupboard under the stairs, neat and ship-shape, we found binoculars, rainproofs and fishing nets.

"Mum can we go to the beach? Can we go fishing? Go on please."

Everyday the children demanded the same picnic. Cottage cheese and peanut butter for Annie. Cheese and cucumber for Josh. Penguins and crisps. They never varied. "Sure you don't want something else Annie? Peanut butter's boring all the time. How about Marmite or some Brie?" But they revelled in the security of regularity, of small routines quickly established. The comfort of predictability.

Loaded with the picnic basket, towels and waterproofs, the nets and buckets from under the stairs, we clambered down the steep footpath to the cove. I thought of the generations of children and parents who'd done the same. Of my grandparents with my father on the beach before the war at Southend-on-Sea, his white legs poking from long worsted shorts and heavy boots, the women with their hair in turbans, huddled under cardigans and rugs in striped deck chairs by the sea wall, as the wind lifted the awning of the Punch and Judy booth and the donkeys carried nervous children across the wet sands. Of me with my parents and Jackie on grey days at Bognor.

The path was fringed with brambles and yellow colts foot, sprinkled with dried sheep pellets. In the wiry grass spongy tufts of pink thrift grew despite the salt spray. To get to the beach we had to climb over large barnacled boulders. In the early spring, when the tides were high, the sea completely covered them, pounding and bashing them into strange shapes. A dog's face. An old man with a bulbous nose. They were wet and slippery under our trainers and sandals.

The beach was empty. The wide wet sand, corrugated by the receding tide, pitted with damp worm casts. Josh rushed down onto the beach and in looping arcs, arms spread wide, wrote **J O S H** in large letters with the handle of his fishing net, staking his claim to the wilderness. Annie took a bucket and went to search rock pools. I joined her and watched as she tried to fish out the tiny transparent shrimps from the miniature submerged cities, before they scurried away in a swirl of watery sand. Fascinated she gently poked glutinous sea anemones until their waving tendrils closed around her stick, collected shells: black mussels and razor bills. "Look Mum, look, look what I've got. Quick. P-l-ease come. Look it's a star fish. I've found a star fish, Josh. Look."

"Here Annie. Let's see. Go on. You lucky thing," he said as we both peered at the brittle astral shape lying in the centre of her small palm. "Well look what I've got," he said draping her with large fronds of green seaweed, trailing it over her shoulders and head like a cloak. "Ugh Josh, you pig, it's all slimy."

By the end of the day their skin was shrivelled. They wouldn't get out of the sea despite their blue lips and chattering teeth. "Just five more minutes," Josh pleaded, diving for the umpteenth time like a dolphin beneath a breaker just before it smashed against the beach. Rough towels. Grit in their shoes and ears.

In the evening, after their baths there was Nivea on sore shoulders, then baked potatoes and Monopoly. Josh was a natural entrepreneur. "Go on Annie, its your go, you're the Boot aren't you? Go on sell me Park Lane. I'll swap you *two* stations and you can have the Old Kent Road," he said planning his future empire of hotels, the vast rents he would accumulate if either of us was unlucky enough to land on his property.

Marion came for a few days. We went to Zennor the day it rained and we couldn't get to the beach, in search of the house D. H. Lawrence had lived in with Frieda. Wrapped in kagools and hoods, the air was thick with sea mist. We had lunch in the pub with thick oak beams where the regulars in their heavy Guernseys stood propped against the bar with their midday pints. Josh took a picture of us drinking the local cider. Then when the clouds cleared we drove on to Bottalack where the tall industrial chimneys of the old tin mines loomed in the spray like an ancient henge perched on the rocks above the Atlantic.

On the Saturday evening Marion and I drank two bottles of Rioja as Josh continued his entrepreneurial extortions on the top bunk with Annie, building a fortune in Mayfair and all the West End sites.

"Hannah, you invest too much in relationships. You *can* have a life alone, develop your work, look after the children. Anyway you're still young, you'll meet someone else. How many years have I been with Derek? God knows, it seems like centuries. We're companionable I suppose, don't argue much, occasionally have sex if we're not too tired and either of us remembers, but honestly, once Jo goes in a few years, I'm not sure that we'll have anything left to say to each other, apart from worrying about what to do with his mother. Sometimes I think we just stay together like a pair old slippers because its easy, what we know. But I can't say I don't have fantasies of my own, of getting up and doing a Freya Stark in my middle age, of disappearing into the hinterland of Mexico, going up the Amazon. Is that the end of the wine? God it's late, I've an early start in the morning. Wish I was staying with you for your last few days."

The night after she left I sat at the window watching the beam of the lighthouse sweep in a milky arc through the small windows. "Mum. Mum. I don't like it when the light goes. When it goes all dark. Mum why isn't Daddy coming? Why does he just love us and not you anymore? I want my Daddy, Mummy," Annie sobbed as she crept into my room and climbed into my bed with her battered panda. And in the morning there were more wet sheets, another wet night-dress. And I thought of Tom waking on those frosty mornings in an icy dormitory to cold water and carbolic soap.

"Did the men really go right under the sea to mine coal?" Josh asked at breakfast.

"Yes I think so. In cages. It was very dangerous. Lots of them drowned. Never came back."

"Like Dad?"

"Not like Dad. He's not dead. He's gone because he wanted to."

"Why?"

"He says he doesn't love me anymore. Josh, I've explained lots of times."

"But he should do. You're our mother."

✳

At first when we get back from Greece everything continues as before. We spend weekends together either at Liam's place or mine. But then almost imperceptibly, he seems to withdraw. "Look I'll see

135

you on Monday, Hannah. Sorry to disappoint the kids. Tell Josh we'll go to the Arsenal game another weekend. I've got to work. Get on. I've already wasted enough time. This bloody play isn't moving fast enough. I need to hold it all together. The strands, the characters. Hear their rhythms of speech. I need to get back to Belfast in my head. The rest is all a distraction."

More and more he seems to retreat into his work as if I'm threatening to steal something from him. I begin to feel like an invader trying to scale the wall of a fortified city. The more I attempt to talk to him the more he shuts down. Slowly, like a ship upping anchor, he seems to slip away. I become fearful of too little and he of too much. In Greece, for a few weeks, we seemed to have found a perfect harmony but now we can't sustain the pitch.

The children's faces become pinched and drawn. Josh scowls and bangs doors, tells me to fuck off over every little thing. Annie sits beside me on the stairs patting my hair with her small ink-stained hands as I sit waiting anxiously for him to phone.

"It's all right Mummy, don't be sad. Please don't be sad. It doesn't matter if Liam and Daddy don't love you any more. You've got me," she says as I bury my face in her lap.

At one in the morning I phone Marion in order not to humiliate myself by phoning Liam. "Hannah, you make yourself too vulnerable. You don't constantly have to seek approval from other people. You set too much store by relationships. Tom, now Liam… Honestly, you expect too much."

And already it is fading. Memories are framed like stills in a film. But they are becoming a memory of the memories. They've been run through my head so often that they're loosing all colour like an over-washed T- shirt. That time when the heating in Liam's flat broke down and I washed my hair in his kitchen sink. He boiled kettles and saucepans to rinse out the soap trying not to scald me or soak the floor, tipping the water over my head until we were both saturated.

Then he licked the suds from my breasts with the tip of his tongue.

This is the first photograph I have of him. Sunday morning by the river in Greenwich near the Royal Naval College. Mist hovering over the gleaming glass and steel of Docklands. We'd been to the Observatory on the hill. Laughing among the Japanese tourists he'd kissed me, his tongue deep in my mouth, as he stood with one foot on either side of the Meridian Line. On Sunday mornings we went to Columbia Road. We'd squeeze through the crowded market, past traders, in from the flat fields of the outlying nurseries of Essex, with their hanging baskets of trailing lobelia, their boxes of red and white busy lizzies and silky-faced pansies. He bought me roses. Not just half a dozen but an armful. Love, looking back, was about excess.

Christmas. We went to buy a tree for the kids. Bundles of mistle-toe and ivy hung from the stalls. Bunches of holly with blood red berries. It was foggy. The air thick with frozen droplets. We drank strong coffee from heavy mugs, ate smoked salmon bagels with cream cheese and spiced applecake in the market café where thawing stall-holders in scarves and jerkins clapped their frozen hands to bring back the circulation. We mingled with the Volvo owners from Barnsbury and Canonbury buying cheap Christmas trees, soaking up a bit of local colour. That night it snowed. The grubby London streets transformed by a pristine whiteness.

"Come here woman, you're freezing," he said pulling me towards him under the duvet, placing my hands in his arm pits, my freezing feet between his thighs while we planned our holiday in Greece. And while he slept, I rang my finger over the birthmark on his chest. Circumnavigating its rocky shoreline, its hidden coves like an explorer searching for a newfoundland.

And I loved him for plaiting Annie's hair in the morning and walking her to school as she chanted her seven times table, leaving me in bed with a cup of tea, and for helping Josh with his maths. They loved him too for his physical solidity, comparing it to my over-anxious chiding. And he was able to do what I'd never managed, to fly the hapless kite. This is my favourite picture. A gusty Saturday afternoon. The kite a blue smudge snaking and twisting high above the Heath, as Liam shows Josh how to pull and manoeuvre the string. Annie is watching wide eyed and beaming. It hurts to see them all together. It's easy for him. They aren't his responsibility. He can walk away.

Until we met, loneliness had been the keynote of my existence. I missed the valley, the smell of apple-wood spluttering in the grate, the drip-drip of the beeches round the cottage when it rained. And I missed Marion. Her ability to take out the sting. Find the balance. Make me laugh at myself, the world, the ridiculous seriousness of it all.

And now there was Tom, waiting, like a general mustering his forces, judging the right moment to attack. Spurred on by Alison, he hides behind solicitor's letters and their blunt-headed language. I'm hardly able to remember what he was like before, to identify any of the things that once drew us together. When I ring to talk about Josh he either slams down the phone or Alison tells me he's out.

I think, in the beginning, Liam was flattered by my interest in his writing. His knowledge of European theatre and poetry, the fact that I was impressed that he could quote great chunks of Neruda by heart. I've always loved books but mine is a visual world. He liked being the expert, teaching me things. But recently I've begun to sense his irritation.

"Hannah, you're so intense. I always have the feeling with you that you're waiting for something more."

"What do you mean? More what?"

"Oh I don't know. Forget it. Just more. You can never just *be*. Everything always has to be so fucking *significant*."

Sunday. It's raining. We've been awake half the night talking in closed chiasmus. For a writer he's never very keen on actual communication. He got up early and is sitting in the kitchen reading for his Monday class. There are dark rings under his eyes. I notice the streaks of grey in his hair.

"You talk too much. You can't leave anything alone. You're like a prodding tongue with toothache. There are other things *apart* from feelings and emotions. Work for example. The world *out there*. Society, ideas. You always have to be engaged in something, analysing, making love. *Relating* – it's such hard work."

"I thought you thought those things were important."

"Of course I do. It's just that I feel, oh I don't know, used up by you. Sometimes I think all this stuff about feelings is a sort of middle class wallowing. If you were unemployed and lived in the Shankhill Road, all you'd have the energy to worry about is where the rent money and the next pint of Guinness was coming from."

"But I love you."

"I know you do," he says softening and coming over from his desk to take my hand "but Hannah it's all too much. I need a bit of space. Things are somehow, what? Oh I don't know... out of balance. We mean different things by 'commitment' and 'relationships'. Look I'm going out."

I try, I really do. To stand still and not lurch towards him as he steps away. Like a dance he take two steps back and I one forward; forever out of sync. But I need him. He gives me colour. Before we met I was transparent as a negative. You could see right through me.

Furtively I start to search his flat, to look in cupboards and kitchen drawers. Not for signs of unfaithfulness as such but for those of independence and withdrawal. A new brand of coffee, a different percolator or a toothbrush? Something that I don't know about that will indicate shift and change? Intimacy is not simply a matter of waking beside someone but knowing the minutiae. What they like on their toast or the time of their next dentist's appointment. I feel the panic mounting as he edges me out. Appointments are made that I don't know about. When I'm away from him I can no longer imagine his day, picture what he's doing. New objects fill the spaces like sea flowing into footprints left on a beach. A different filing cabinet, a new mug in the bathroom. I start to search his drawers, his bathroom cabinet. What am I looking for? Condoms? Another woman's toothbrush? There's a new expensive bottle of Yves St. Laurent aftershave I'd never seen before. Hay fever tablets, an old bottle of Kaolin and Morphine, the usual shaving things. His life is running on without me. And I haven't been into the darkroom for weeks.

Secrets. Secrets. I remember how as a child I'd searched through the drawers of my mother's dressing table, through my father's desk. What had I been looking for then? What am I looking for now?

Ironically I think Liam is more like Tom than I realised. Not abandoned as a child to a succession of whiskery aunts but smothered by his mother's need of him as her only child in that small Belfast terrace. He has never blamed her. How could he? She only wanted the best for him, for him to follow in his father's footsteps after the shooting. Leave for the safety of a university in England or Dublin. Become a teacher like him. "She's a good woman, Hannah," he says protectively. I wish he would introduce us but he never has. I like her face. Soft, old fashioned, hair caught in a neat bun at the nape of her neck in the photo he keeps on his desk. She is a midwife. A woman of faith. Maybe the fact that he has never introduced us makes me realise that he doesn't really love me enough or that the emotional responsibility for two women is just too much. I feel absurdly jealous of his past loves. Of Claire, with whom he grew up and lived all through university, from tom-boy to Joni Mitchell waif. She knew his mother. His mother loved her, he told me, hoped they would marry. There was always a bond between them he says, like mother and daughter. Perhaps it's just that there's

140

something restless about him, an inability to carry anything through. For in the end he left her to go off and travel. Nepal, India, Thailand. Just as I know he is going to leave me.

"I'll drive you down to Claygate to pick up the kids," Liam says suddenly one Sunday afternoon when I have to go and get Josh and Annie from my parents. He is intrigued to meet them. Instinctively I don't want him to. Don't want them to be able, one day to add him, like a notch, to a counting-stick of my failures. But he comes anyway.

He's impressed by the house. The antiques and watercolours, the deep comfortable sofas. I'm taken aback. Where is his much vaunted revolutionary zeal?

"They're quite nice really," you say as we drive back to London, the children laden with sweets and money.

And I know what he's thinking. That I had a privileged childhood, hadn't had to struggle against poverty, become the man of the house at ten. That I'd had it, by his lights, easy. How could my anxieties to placate my father, to know my roots and discover where I belonged, in any way compare to the hardships of a small boy looking after a distraught mother too traumatised by the shooting of her husband to go beyond the corner shop? He'd enjoyed the civilised Sunday lunch, my mother's roast beef, my father's Beaujolais Nouveau, the papers and coffee with a little Mozart, the habitual walk. My father had told him, almost as soon as he'd got through the door, that Jackie's husband, Steve, had just been offered a partnership with his firm. And my mother had taken to him, I could see, as they both threw sticks for the dogs. Rufus kept running back to him. Liver ears flapping, slobbering with excitement. He had a knack. I felt a bit betrayed. While I helped her put out the tea cups on a tray and the walnut and coffee cake she had made especially, she clucked approving noises. "A very charming young man Hannah. I don't usually like a Northern Irish accent, I must say, rather harsh, but he seems very charming, very cultivated." We drive back to

London in silence, the kids picking up the tension, squabbling in the back of the car. And I know that he's jealous, jealous that despite my insecurities, my lack of self-worth that I didn't have to live in a sad dark terrace against a backdrop of violence, making do.

After that he doesn't ring for two weeks. I can't stand it. In the end I simply called at the flat. It's nearly ten o'clock by the time I pluck up the courage. I feel sick walking up the concrete stairwell I've come to know so well. I know it's stupid, that he'll see it as an intrusion. But I can't help myself. I'm overwhelmed by the need to talk, to touch him. Through the half drawn curtains I can see him sitting by the gas fire, naked from the waist, in a pair of old jeans, listening to music on head phones. On the floor there are two glasses. An empty bottle of wine. Cigarette papers. Some spent spliffs.

He doesn't want to let me in. An unfamiliar leather jacket is hanging on the back of the chair. My eyes try to avoid the bed. It's unmade. The sheets crumpled.

"Hannah this is not a good idea. It's not really very convenient. I've got Claire staying. She's in a play at the Gate. She's over from Belfast and had nowhere to stay. She'll be back after the performance."

And I can smell it. The smell of sex. The scent of another woman on him.

He never comes right out with it. Water gurgles through the pipes of the house like a pulse. The phone assumes mystical properties. The flick of eight little buttons, the space of thirty seconds and I could hear his voice, bring him, however fleetingly, back into my life. For minutes, hours, days I will myself not to go near it as it taunts me across the room. I won't phone. I won't tell him how much I need him, hand him that power.

But in the end, of course, I do.

"Oh Hannah hi! Actually this isn't a very good moment. I'm just literally on my way out. The BBC. I'm going to a meeting. There's a chance of a new script. Yes. It's great isn't it. How are you? The kids? Look I'll call back when I have a minute but I'm really tied up just now."

Lies. Lies. Humiliation burns my cheeks. I want to scream. To force him to tell me the truth, to say the words. Force him to tell me that it's over.

My loneliness is the colour of lilac. Dark as a bruise, deep as the shadows under flower pots. It is the colour of sick rooms smelling of camphor and enamel bowls, of old flannel. It clings to my skin with its own particular sour odour. I avoid other people. The only person I speak to is Marion. Long, long conversations on the phone, when she listens, hardly speaking, patiently flicking curls of ash into the lid of her cigarette packet on the other end of the line.

Everywhere I look for clues and omens. The world becomes encoded with secret signs. I buy the newspapers to read my horoscope, create charms and strange formulae. If I add his telephone number to the date and it is even, then he'll come back. If I pass two magpies in the park then he'll come back. But only a solitary bird pecks by the bench as I force myself to go for a walk past the sandpit where pregnant mothers stand chatting as their toddlers play.

There is nothing except an infinite silence and my part of our unfinished conversation unwinding, again and again, like an answerphone tape in my head. Days lap around my ankles like the tide, coming in and in. I sit in my bedroom with the copy of the *I Ching* I bought years ago in Oxford in a bookshop near Magdalen bridge, throwing hexagram after hexagram, trying to find some pattern in the esoteric hieroglyphics.

24 Fu – Return: The Turning Point, The Receptive Earth, The Arousing Thunder.

After the time of decay comes the turning point. The powerful light that has been banished returns.

143

I know I can make it mean whatever I want, that I'm no longer being rational.

✳

"Jennifer," I lie. "My name's Jennifer."

"Don't be worried. I won't tell you anything to frighten you. Come at 10.00. I charge £25. The top bell."

The voice is hard to identify. Mittel European? I'm shaking as I get off the Central Line at Queensway. Can I really be doing this? It seems such a cliché. In the past I've always read horoscopes with a mixture of childish wish-fulfilment and irony. I know I'm grabbing at straws. The streets are full of people going to work or window shopping. Racks of newspapers in Arabic, German, French spill onto the pavement from newsagents whose windows display postcards for busty blondes and stern governesses. The window of a French pâtisserie is piled with glazed strawberry *tartes*, cream-filled *éclairs* and *milles feuilles*. Delicacies for jaded Middle Eastern shoppers who live and work in the Embassies around. The smell of coffee draws me in. I'm early so order a cappuccino.

On the next table are a mother and daughter out shopping. Italian perhaps? With those soft leather jackets and impossible stiletto heels. A young Scandinavian couple with a large rucksack sit in a corner pawing over a map. But it is the woman in red who catches my eye, with her ink-black hair pulled straight back from her brow and tied in a loop at the nape of her neck. Nothing about her is real. Neither the colour of her hair nor the carefully pencilled brows drawn in place of those she lacks or the exaggerated crimson bow of her lips. She wears a red suit with black trims and brass buttons like a matador's bolero. A Chanel suit, fashionable some twenty years ago. She's very thin and her skin hangs under her chin in papery folds like creased parchment, while her liver-spotted hands with their scarlet nails flutter restlessly like speckled moths over her immaculate hair. She orders another black coffee from the young waiter whom she calls by his first name. She must be a regular. She is so carefully dressed, yet apparently has nowhere else to go. When the coffee arrives she takes out a cigarette and waits for him to light it, as if extending the whole episode to create a small brush-stroke of colour on the blank canvas of her day.

Madame Florrie answers the door wearing pink track suit bottoms, trainers and a floral housecoat. Her hennaed hair is orange as an orangoutang's. Small and dumpy she must be about seventy. She's not what I'd expected.

"Ah Jennifer? You are early. Vill you vait a little?"

Her accent is heavy, a sort of cartoon English, which she seems to speak only with great effort. She shows me into her cramped sitting room. Most of the space is taken up by the vast TV screen. The bookshelf houses rows of videos: *Gone with the Wind*, *The Sound of Music*. Heart-shaped frames enclose photographs of what I presume to be grandchildren and various smiling, no doubt satisfied, couples. A cut glass vase of plastic roses stands on a lace crochet cloth in the centre of a low gilt table. Elaborate net curtains hang in grimy festoons at the window. Jennifer, I think, panicking. I must remember Jennifer.

A few minutes later she leads me into her bedroom. In the corner is a slightly crumpled bed and two chairs. In between them she has placed a kitchen stool to act as a table. Mauve draylon curtains are drawn against the mid-morning sun and a flounced nylon cover has been pulled unevenly over the bed. A smell of cheap rose talcum powder fills the room.

"Sit down." Her voice is soft, coaxing.

"Here take these – you play cards?" I shake my head, "Never mind. You can shuffle?" she says handing me a pack of playing cards. I pick them up and mix them inexpertly.

"Now cut the deck into three with your left hand. That's right," she encourages as I continue to shuffle ineptly. I never play cards, except Snap or Happy Families with the kids on holiday in Cornwall when it's too wet to go out because the air is so thick with rain from the Atlantic that even the sheep huddle for shelter behind stone walls.

I place the cards on the stool between us and she begins to lay them out in an intricate formation that I can't follow. A few minutes pass while she seems to be studying the result. I've no idea what she's looking for.

"You are not happy." I don't reply. It seems a fair guess. Presumably few new clients come to see her when their lives are going well.

"Someone is making you sad?"

Again I say nothing. I don't want to give myself away; anyway she can work it out for the money. I wonder why I didn't given her my real name, presented a false personae. Still if she is genuine she'll tell me why I'm here without my feeding her titbits. If not, I'll know that I've wasted my money. Anyway I don't believe in things like this.

"In three months things will be better for you." She says continuing to lay out the pack "...and you will be alright financially."

I try to follow her reading. Diamonds for money, clubs for career ..."you will have some success in you career, you will see" ...and hearts, hearts for love. The numbers on the cards are presumably the date and the time.

"This person who is making you sad does care about you but they are muddled and upset. They do not know what to do. They are not as strong as you. Yes. Yes. You see," she says turning up another heart, "there is not doubt they are bothered inside." Her words are like a slap in the face. "Stronger than you." Tears of anger begin to well as I imagine you in your room in front of your old typewriter

146

(you continue to balk at technology), trying to shut out the world, bury your confusion. And I sense the anger and scepticism you would express if you knew that I was resorting to something as superstitious and irrational as this.

"You are a creative person?" I nod, but suppose that everyone feels this in some way. Feels the potential, even if it's shrivelled or dormant, never acted upon. "Yes, I can see that and very passionate, (is this just flattery, telling me what she suspects I might want to hear?) I think this man – we are talking about a man aren't we? – is frightened by that." And as she speaks, your words come hurtling back. "I feel used up by you Hannah," and I shudder.

With the drawn curtains and the heavy rosy scent the room is beginning to feel claustrophobic. I've hardly said a word. As if by keeping quiet I can pretend that I'm not really here, fool myself that it is merely an accident that I am sitting in this old woman's stuffy bedroom in the middle of Bayswater on a Wednesday morning. Rowed on a shelf above the bed is a collection of plaster saints in candied pinks and blues. There is the Lord's prayer painted on a porcelain plaque beside an Arabic text which has been propped next to a Russian icon. And suddenly I'm in another room, filled with icons and the sound of piano music, and another old woman displaced by upheaval and political chaos. Finally I pluck up courage and ask where she's from.

"From Lithuania. Via Egypt. I came here as a young girl. You know, the war," she says as if that explains everything. "I have had psychic powers since I was seven."

I try to picture her in Alexandria before the war. A teeming city of dark doorways and beaded curtains, of rose-water, of hidden courtyards and cool fountains, and I wonder what secret things she witnessed as a girl, how she discovered that she had powers to see into the deep wells of other's sadness.

"Well Jennifer, you want I tell you how to get him back?" I nod, for a moment believing she might just be able to do that. "You have a Bible?" I shake my head. Not since school assemblies, too scared to say the Lord's prayer out loud in case a bolt from heaven struck my blasphemous Jewish head, had I had a Bible.

"You have his photograph, ugh?" I pull out the one Annie took that Sunday on Hampstead Heath. Liam is sitting on the grass. I'm crouching behind him, laughing, my arms around his neck.

"Good. Nice. You look nice together," she says examining it.

Then she opens a white leather Bible, flipping through the Psalms until she gets to the Song of Songs. "Ah this is good: *While I slept, my heart was awake, I dreamt my lover knocked at the door.* See how it ends: *My lover is mine and I am his.* Now you read this every night. You start tomorrow. Tonight is not good. You have candles? You need nine red candles. You light one every night and read this and hold the photograph and think of your lover. Then close your eyes and imagine yourself in a beautiful place. Always the same place mind. Don't change it and imagine him coming to you."

Outside the streets are a mist of drizzle. The swish and drone of traffic in the busy rush of Bayswater. The daylight hurts my eyes after the shaded room. I feel exhausted. On the way to the tube I go into the supermarket and buy a box of red candles. I hold them tight all the way to Bethnal Green, trying to dismiss the voice of reason, trying to believe that I have the power to will Liam back. That night I do nothing, but the next I lock my bedroom door, draw the blinds and set the candles on the table next to a small incense burner of sandalwood oil. I burn the candles for five nights, clutching the photo in one hand and Annie's school Bible in the other and picture him walking across the beach towards me, the sun glinting in his hair, as I wait for him in the shade of the taverna on a deserted beach. And as the candles gutter and flicker, I recite the ancient psalm, willing him to come to me, willing him to take away the hurt.

On the sixth day I stop. Throw away the oil, bin the rest of the candles, and tear up the photo. I can't believe I am doing this. I'm losing my reason. I know he is never coming back.

＊ ·

Dawn. I can't sleep and lie listening to the patter of rain, the chatter of damp birds. The morning is grey as iron outside the window. My pyjamas are rucked around my middle and in that hinterland between sleep and waking I'm dreaming again. I am in the woods, in the valley below the cottage. I've lost the children. I call their names again and again only to hear my voice muffled by the thick vegetation, caught on the jagged hawthorn.

At breakfast my head is befuddled as I get their toast and they rush round getting ready for school. As they leave I decide to go to the park and try and get some air before going into the darkroom, put some distance between the morning and my dreams. I pull on a track-suit and scuffed trainers. The rain seems to have stopped. I turn down Approach Road to Victoria Park where I pass what I assume to be a cast of regulars. A tattooed man in a purple shell-suit accompanied by a muzzled alsatian, a young black runner, his polished mahogany muscles glistening with sweat as he jogs round the lake deafened by a walkman. On the water a group of drakes is gang-banging a lone duck in a flurry of flapping and squawking. Two elderly Bengalis sit under astrakhan hats chatting on a bench and I wonder how Della is. I haven't seen her for days. I wonder if she'll really have the courage to leave Dave.

It is still early. The ice-cream stand is boarded up. Torn wrappers scud across the gravel. I think of Josh and Annie, their small faces smeared custard yellow on a summer's afternoon. Josh used to bring his skateboard here when we first came to London. Now we hardly ever come to the park.

It begins to spit with rain again. I circle the lake and go back via the corner shop as I've run out of coffee. In the flat I plug in the kettle and go to the bathroom and turn on the shower. Above the sink, in the speckled mirror, I catch sight of my still sleep-worn face. I'm shocked. The freshness is no longer automatic. Now it has to be worked at, wooed. It seems that at each stage of my life, just as I am becoming used to it, my body transmutes into something unfamiliar.

I strip off and climb beneath the steaming faucet, closing my eyes as hot water cascades over my shoulders, between my thighs. I pour a dollop of pine gel into my palm. A webbed tracery of silver lines maps my breasts and stomach. When pregnant with Josh my skin stretched taut as a drum. My breasts swelled to twice their normal size. Annie's insistent heel nearly finished my bladder.

Yet youth is what I am used to. I'm familiar with the intimacy of men's gaze. Sitting opposite them on the tube, the narrowing of their gimlet eyes. I know the games. Whether to turn away my head and freeze them out, or to hold, a moment longer than is necessary, a pair of hazel eyes before I falter to shift attention to my own distorted window-reflection.

Now I begin to notice them everywhere. In bus queues, in the newsagents buying scratch cards or in the supermarkets laden with shopping. The invisible women. With their crimped grey hair and wrinkled paper skin. Narrowed lips corrugated into a delta of lines flooded with a stain of lipstick. Flat sensible shoes. Clothes for covering the body, for comfort, not for emphasising the curve of a touchable breast or thigh. Sensible M&S pleats and British Home Stores easy-care-polyester. Just pop in on a low temperature. Wash and drip dry. No fuss. No bother. Saves time. For what? Satins, peach-coloured silks and lace camisoles need care. Imply expectation. An audience.

My skin is burning. I lather my legs and reach for the razor. I haven't shaved them for weeks. At what moment do you decide that there's no point in that black net underwired bra, those matching cut away briefs? Stop shaving unseen legs. Understand that there'll be no more slow unbuttonings in the candle light. The frisson of flesh on flesh.

I climb out of the shower and wrap myself in a large rough towel. White foam clings to the back of my legs, my neck. I shake my head and stick it back under the tap, there are still suds in my ears. Then I towel myself dry. Outside the street is beginning to fill with the chatter of children on the way to school, the clink of milk bottles and I am filled with a sense of loss for how it might have been. I didn't realise love was so inarticulate. So obdurate.

✳

It is 2 am. Suddenly the phone rings snatching me brutally from sleep. Anxiety permeates the thin film of consciousness. An accident? Has Josh been hurt? He told me he was staying the night at his friend Sam's. Through the rattan blinds the sodium glare from the street lamp curdles in a sickly pool on the floor.

"What is it, what's the matter? Is my son all right?" I ask, my limbs lacking co-ordination as I fumble for the bedside light.

"Your son, Madam, was picked up in Dalston carrying a quantity of drugs. Perhaps you'd like to come and collect him."

"Drugs? What drugs? But my daughter? What time is it? There's no one else here… I can't leave her on her own."

"Well," the voice is off-hand, uninterested in the maternal logistics, "someone will have to come and get him. He can't stay here."

Can I drive there and back and leave Annie asleep? I need to phone and tell someone. But there is no one to tell. Caught between my children's needs, I decide to risk it. I creep out of bed and pull on my jeans from the compost of clothes on the floor. A sweater, boots, whatever I can find. The house reverberates to its own silence with

Annie the small breathing nucleus at its centre. I'm not sure of the way as I drive through empty streets that are as black and desolate as I feel. This is what I have feared. I haven't known what to do about the tell-tale plastic bags, the cigarette papers and foil, the stray threads of dried grass. I tried to hold down the panic, to talk to him, to find the right tone. But he has become furtive. Taken to leaving his windows open. But I know that sweet thick smell. The sign above a mini-cab office bleeds its flashing neon onto the wet pavement. Three young rastas stand silhouetted in the doorway of a 24 hour kebab house. Josh is slipping out of my reach beyond the safe territory of childhood. He refuses to get up in the morning, to visit Tom, is withdrawn and morose. What has happened to the boy who only a summer ago ran free as a wet labrador on an empty beach? Perhaps I made a mistake leaving the country. The winding lanes where the damp greenness smelt of wild garlic. Nothing holds us here, pins us into the fabric of this city. The warp and weft is unwinding. Liam's leaving has hurt Josh too. A double betrayal. Josh enjoyed having a man around again. The shaving foam, the bristle brush and Gillette razor left in my bathroom were symbolic allies in a house of women. 'Mum you don't know *an-y-thing*' he moaned when I tried to take an interest after the two of them had returned from a match at Highbury with bags of vinegary chips, trailing red and white scarves.

Dacre Street. Dallington Street. Dalston... I stop the car. The crammed names in the A-Z swim in a blur beneath the street lamp.

"Someone'll be down in a minute. Take a seat." The duty officer barely lifts his eyes from the sports page and his mug of tea. He is in shirt sleeves, his thick arms covered with a sandy gilding of fur. The blue shirt is drawn taught across his protruding gut. Handcuffs, keys, a two-way radio hang from his belt. Above the filing cabinet an electric clock buzzes into the silence.

I sit and wait on the bench reading the posters for rape-lines and for those who have been victims of violent crime. "Come through.

I'll get your son," announces another officer, sticking his head round the door, after twenty distraught minutes of waiting.

He unlocks the heavy iron door of a cell. Josh is slumped on a bench in a corner. Along the passageway a drunk is swearing and banging on the wall to be let out.

"Joshy!" His face is grey as putty. His eyes heavy and red-rimmed, the corners gummed with sleep, as the officer steers him unsteadily by the elbow. I want to reach out to hold him. To bridge the gap between this pale young man and the small boy who used to squelch through the mud at my side collecting eggs in a white basin. But I do nothing.

"Hello Mum," he murmurs sheepishly looking at the floor. On the desk is the release form. Beneath the shade of a black angle-poise a moth is diving again and again into the hot bulb.

His eyes won't meet mine as the officer cautions him, explains, that as this is a first offence, someone will come to the house and talk to him. "Do you understand?" he asks, turning to Josh who simply nods. Suddenly he looks very vulnerable inside his street-wise black nylon bomber jacket.

As we step into the night the damp air catches in the back of my throat. "Don't you ever, ever do anything like this to me again," I scream shaking him violently by the shoulders, the tension in me snapping as I burst into sobs and we stand on the steps of the Police Station bleached by the blue of the station lamp. "Don't you realise how worried I've been. I've had to leave Annie on her own…" And before I can finish he is off, over the zebra crossing, past the kebab house, the block of flats, across the forecourt of the 24 Hour Shell garage. Nearly hysterical, I run back into the station. But the duty sergeant with the gingery arms simply shrugs as he glances up from the sports page, annoyed at another interruption, saying that Josh is now my responsibility, that he has been released into my care.

Shaking I drive up and down endless anonymous terraced

streets, peering into dripping gardens, damp bus shelters and empty doorways. I can't leave Annie on her own much longer, she might wake. As I pull up to the curb outside the flat, Josh is sitting in a soaked huddle on the door step. I leap out of the car not knowing whether to hit or hug him and flop down wearily by his side. His trainers are spattered with mud. I put my arm around him and his head sinks into my shoulder. We are both crying. The hard muscular body under his jacket feels unfamiliar. I can't remember the last time he let me touch him. I can't pinpoint the moment of physical separation when he no longer felt it appropriate to come into my room in the morning, climb onto the end of the bed with his home-work or comic. I think of how we had sat together, in those first months, in his room high in the eaves of the cottage, his snub nose covered in milk spots, snuffling at my breast, as the dawn rain dripped in the beeches. A life stretching ahead. His hair smells unwashed like the fur of a damp dog. And in his tear-stained features I see a trace of Tom's vanished face.

※

I can remember a young woman in Sainsburys, by the frozen food cabinet, grabbing her small boy by the hand and dumping him roughly in a push chair, telling him that it was rude to stare. Other people gathered like spectators at a crash. Everything was a blur. All I could see was this badge saying *Terry* looming in front of me. It had a nose covered with opened pores and dark hairs. "No need to worry love, ambulance's on its way."

Now everything is white. White and clean. Except the orange whorls on the cubicle curtains that suck me in like molten orbs. Starched linen and sick bowls. I can't smell my body anymore. The smell of cleanliness has wrapped itself around the other smells. Piss, vomit, shit.

154

The thermometer reads 70F. But I'm shivering. The mirror above the sink glints like the lens of a fish eye. The floor is polished linoleum, a silver lake. I want to swim out into it, on and on, my platinum body, my sequinned fins twisting and turning beneath the icy water. I want to swim off into the clear arctic wastes, the ice floes of the north, searching for new continents. On past the solitary whalers and sealers, the tall masted ships, where their rigging freezes like glass and the Aurora Borealis electrifies the dark.

A fly buzzes trapped in the frosted light shade. It has got in but it can't get out. A nurse comes in and slips a mercury bulb between my lips then takes my pulse. Her arms are freckled, wrapped above the elbow in frilled white cuffs like lamp chops in a French restaurant. A small watch balances on the shelf of her bosom.

"And what's your name then, dear?"

I don't answer but sit silently unpicking the stained trim of the blanket so that suddenly I am back in the rear of the Humber next to Jackie, fingering the satin binding on the tartan rug across our knees. In the front I can hear the drone of adult voices. Telegraph wires flash by as we play the game of being the first to spot a cow, a pub, a red telephone box. There are buckets and spades, a lilo and the wicker picnic hamper fitted with green bakelite plates and cups on the back shelf. Our small voices are insistent "Are we there yet? Are we nearly there? I was first, Mummy. I was the first to see the sea." Outside the hospital window is a garden with rose beds. A groundsman is raking the grass.

I want my own night-dress. Someone has taken my clothes. There is a red welt where the starched rim of the gown they have given me has chaffed my neck. The arm pits are stained with marks the colour of weak tea. I sit watching the groundsman cover the flowerbeds with straw-filled manure. He goes backwards and forwards filling a wheel barrow from the back of a lorry The roses are pruned so severely that there are no leaves, just bare sticks. The hospital

155

grounds are neat as the municipal crematoria crammed between straggling allotments I pass on the Waterloo line when I take the train to my parents. And all the time, in my head, I can hear the sound of the waterfall, smell the lane filled with wild garlic and sorrel.

Group therapy sessions. They say it will do me good. I am supposed to go twice a week. In the day room there are a couple of dusty rubber plants, some bright holiday posters of fishing boats on the Costa del Sol, a smiling white-toothed girl playing beach-ball in a bikini. Are these images supposed to be something to aim for, enforced proof of normality? The upright chairs sit huddled against the walls like nervous children. The green corridors are decorated with soft-focus water-colours of swans and Alpine scenes. Nothing that will jar. Unhappiness it seems is supposed to make you soggy-brained. Down the hall old ladies shuffle to the toilet on mottled legs, their purple feet swamped in baggy slippers.

I attend twice but can't bear it, the weight of other people's misery when it's hard enough to bear my own. Then out of the blue Marion rings.

"Honestly Hannah, I didn't know. Your mother phoned. She wanted to talk to me about the children. Look I've got a few days leave. I'll come up and stay. I might even fit in a trip to the National. They're doing Vanya. You know me and Chekhov. Also there's something I need to give you."

She arrives at the flat with pasta and two bottles of Rioja. As she cooks I soak in a bath. When I get out she has set the kitchen table with a clean checked cloth, put fresh candles in the holders and opened the wine. As I pull out a chair she pours me a glass then slips an envelope across the table in my direction. I recognise the writing at once.

"Hannah, I've had this for a while now. I wasn't sure what to do with it as it's addressed to me but I think, on balance, you should see it. I didn't want to show it to you before, to add to your worries. I hope you won't think I've been meddling. You know, don't you, that I care about you, that I just thought it might help."

I stare at it for a moment, unable to open it. Still no word processor. That familiar type with its uneven jumping *r* and the weight of it like lead in my lap. I drain my glass of Rioja in one, then pour out another and read the letter.

Home Farm, Galloway

Dear Marion,

Thank you for your letter. I, in fact, received it several days ago and have been carrying it round with me ever since, uncertain how I should respond. Perhaps it's cowardice that I haven't done so before. I will be honest, my instinct was to ignore it. Always the easiest solution. For I sense, that whatever I write will inevitably sound like a justification, and maybe, in truth, it is. I was, of course, very distressed to hear about Hannah, but – does it sound callous? – not altogether surprised.

You say that she keeps asking for me. That you feel if I were to come and see her in hospital, it might help her recovery. For a moment, my own sense of guilt – that I am somehow responsible for her breakdown – nearly got the better of me and I was going to drive to the airport and get on a plane. But they were all booked for the next 48 hours and the longer I thought about it, the less convinced I became that it was the right thing to do. For I feel, in my bones, that only when Hannah finally accepts that I am not coming back, will she ever start to get better. To come to London now would only be to give her false hope, hope for something that is not going to happen. Yet as I write, to you, a complete stranger, I am aware that all this is so much rationalisation, that in the end, each of us does what we want and

157

need to do. No, I am not, not coming back to see Hannah because I think it will harm her, but because I think it will harm me.

It was not easy to leave her. I do hope you believe that. It was not something I did casually. I knew she would take it badly. Not because it was me who was leaving but because she experienced it, I suppose, as compounding all the other losses in her life. I realised, after a while, that I could never give her what she needed. Could not be what she thought I was, had constructed as the fantasy, of the man she wanted, in her head.

When I first saw her in the bookshop it was, of course, that striking hair I noticed first. That sprung copper wire. She never thought of herself as beautiful. She didn't have enough confidence. She seldom smiled and when she did, it was like something learnt. But it was the depth of her sadness that drew me. Dark, somehow unreachable. She always saw herself as an outsider. I think that's what drew her to the East End. A spurious connection with a past that when she started searching, she realised no longer existed. She had this great need to belong, as though it was a condition that could be arrived at through sheer endeavour. I think it's what also took her to Somerset with Tom. A desire to put down roots. Jewish angst, she used to joke. Her Russian ancestry showing through. Despite the middle class accoutrements, her family were, she always claimed, really escapees from a Woody Allen film. Take away the wax Barbours and the dogs, she'd laugh, and they'd start flinging their hands in the air and beating their foreheads with their palms and crying Oy Vey! Actually I met them once and they seemed perfectly nice to me. But then one never really knows what goes on in families.

They hated her living in Bethnal Green, I know that. The studio, the kids' school. I don't think they had a clue what she was trying to do. She would get in such a state after one of her mother's phone calls. Putney or Fulham would have been more their cup of tea. Green spaces, middle class kids. You know the sort of thing. I know Josh was starting to get a bit wild. But I've always thought the kids were fine. But what do I know about these things? I miss them though. Josh and I were good mates. I used to take him to the football at Highbury.

I admire that about Hannah though, she didn't take the easy way out. But she has something of a talent for pain. She simply couldn't accept that her sadness was ordinary, part of the human condition. It made her feel guilty. She was good at guilt and I'm the one who was raised a Catholic!

As you can imagine, I've been over and over all this a thousand times in my head. I think much of the reason she was attracted to me in the first place was Belfast. Her idea of Belfast at least. I became, for her, if it doesn't sound too far fetched, a sort of romantic hero. Someone who could understand suffering, someone who had an affinity with death. Suffering fascinated her. She always thought I was the strong one. The reality, for me, of course was very different. I left as soon as I could. Perhaps she told you about that. About my Dad. The irony was he always tried to be above politics. Children, teaching, were what mattered to him. So my memories of Belfast are hardly glamorous. Life was hard enough as a boy trying to hold my mother together. She had been a midwife. Enlightened, progressive, in a city of too many births. Hannah always wanted to meet her but somehow it never seemed right. So you see my Ulster is not one of resistance, of banners and parades, but of trips to change my mother's library book. Perhaps that's how I ended up a writer. I used to stay at the library as long as I could before going home. I did very little in those years except work. My Belfast was 7' by 8'. A universe I inhabited with Ché Guevara and Joan Baez.

It seems very strange thinking about all this, sitting here writing to you – someone I've never met – from the peace of my uncle's farm. As I look out of the window the wet fields are dotted with black and white cows. I'm afraid I've completely narrowed my focus. As the Bard says 'The play's the thing', and I've just had a possible offer from Channel

4 and have another eight weeks to get it finished. Fashionable stuff now, I suppose if I'm cynical, a Belfast childhood. It feels good here. Damp earth and mist. I help around the farm to justify my keep. Do a bit of the milking.

Forgive me Marion. This is becoming rambling and self-obsessed. I suppose, partly, it's an attempt to offer an explanation, because, in the end I am saying to you, no I can't come. I was drowning under the weight of Hannah's need or so it felt. I did, I think, honestly love her, if, indeed, I am capable of such an emotion but it was never enough. She always seemed to want more. I felt dried up. I'm safer nowadays with art. But Hannah believes in relationships. For her it is a primary form of creativity. In the end, I suppose, I am not prepared or able to change. And then there is Claire. We've been seeing each other again from time to time, nothing fixed, nothing solid, but the ties go a long way back.

I hope, Marion, you will not judge me too harshly, that this does not sound too callous. But I cannot help Hannah. I am glad she has you with her. I really do wish her well and hope she is out of hospital soon. Next time I'm over, perhaps I could buy you a drink by way of saying thank-you.

With best wishes,
Liam O'Farrell.

A fist closes and opens in my stomach. I cannot take my eyes from the letter, from the intimacy and immediacy of his signature, as if it might by some mystical means communicate something beyond its mere physical presence on the page. I don't know what to feel, whether this sudden stab of pain belongs to the moment, here and now, sitting in my kitchen with my friend drinking wine, or if it is a residual emotion, simply a delayed reaction, like shock, something that should have been felt when the letter was originally written.

160

The knowledge that he's with Claire feels like a bruise in my side. Was I then simply an interlude, an entr'acte to the main event? For weeks I have yearned for his touch, for the smell of him, familiar as home. But I know now, what perhaps before I had not faced, that he is not coming back. The evidence is sitting in my lap.

I can't sleep. All night I lie under the Madonna's wings drifting in and out of dreams. Yet it is not Liam I dream of but as usual the children. I wake terrified that I have lost them again. In my sleep I call and call their names across the valley, search for them in the woods, down by the waterfall as I have done night after night. But there is never any answer. I wake in a panic that there is no one left in my life.

"Come on Hannah, what you need is to get out. Some fresh air. You have got to stop living inside your head."

And Marion is right. We go for a short walk to Victoria Park and sit in the café by the lake and drink hot chocolate as the ducks bob for stale bread. A couple of boys playing truant from school are trying to sink a Coke can with a stick. The sky is cold and grey, the pale sun the colour of coddled egg. We walk arm in arm around the lake enjoying the easy warmth of old friendship.

"Marion, are the kids all right? I've been worried sick about them. And Tom, I'm frightened of Tom."

"They're fine Hannah. I managed to have a word with Josh when your mother phoned. He asked if you were all right. What had happened. I don't think your mother has told him much, which I don't think has helped. I just said that you were very tired and had been in hospital for a rest and that he wasn't to worry. He sent his love. Annie seems fine. We had quite a chat. Apparently Tom and Alison are going down to take them out for the weekend."

"Marion, I miss them. I can't bear it if Tom..."

"Come on. Thinking like that won't help. I'll buy you lunch. I'm starving and it's time you ate something. Do you fancy a curry?"

161

So we catch a bus to Brick Lane. In the restaurant the walls are covered with murals of doe-eyed Indian maidens with tiny waists cavorting in an exotic garden.

"Anything you don't want or shall I just order?"

We eat Nan stuffed with almonds and garlic, vegetable biryani and dhal washed down with salty lassie. It's the first time I've enjoyed food for weeks. Hot lime pickle, sweet mango chutney, the massala poppadums.

"Marion. How do you do it? Always know the right thing to do?"

After we have eaten we wander round Whitechapel. Up Fournier Street and Princelet Street. At the Hawksmoor church I stop and see if Mary is there. But there is no sign. Then despite our large lunch we pop into the deli and that evening at my kitchen table, where Annie and I once baked bread, we talk and talk about the past, about books and our children, about Chekov and photography and sex, until I feel something inside me begin to melt. Slowly the ashtray fills with a pyramid of Marion's cigarette butts as we finish the second bottle of wine and I know that I have started the long haul back.

✳

The day begins with the usual rushed routine. Josh refuses to get out of bed. I, as always, am anxious and chivvying as he crashes his mountain bike out of the door with only a few minutes to spare, his blazer stuffed into his rucksack, his tie creased into his pocket. Too old now for packed lunches, he has chips at the corner shop and cans of Coke with his mates in the park.

Annie's more organised. Everything is arranged methodically in her pencil case, she always has her music for her recorder class. She seems to make sure that the world is braced and scaffolded around her. But I worry about her in the city, walking to school alone through these East London streets among the drunks, the down-and-outs, the flotsam and jetsam.

I stand frozen in the hallway, in the silence imprinted with their shapes, unable to move, the letter burning in my fingers. The stained-glass birds and branches of apple blossom in the front door seep coloured light onto the wood floor. An unopened telephone bill and a flyer for free pizzas lie on the mat by Annie's bike. And I think of her in her pram under the lilac tree as Josh and I planted leathery broad beans in the vegetable patch. "Can these be my own beans Mum? Can they please?"

Everything is unravelling like snagged knitting My chest is tight as though someone has squeezed out all the air. I sit down on the bottom stair and read and re-read the letter again:

...have only just heard that you have been in hospital. I found out from your mother when she phoned to ask if I could have the children. Apparently they have been with her. I cannot say that I am surprised by what I have heard. It is something I have long expected. It was, quite frankly, only a matter of time. The fact is, that your irrational insistence, against my advice and wishes, that Josh and Annie should live with you in the East End, has done nothing but harm. But the truth is not something you welcome.

And that truth is, that you have been an unmitigated disaster for my children both emotionally and educationally. Because of your self-absorption, your lack of supervision, Josh is in danger of getting involved with the wrong crowd. He is falling behind with his education and I do not feel confident of your ability to cope any better with Annie at this vulnerable point in her growing up. This is not, as I am sure you will try and claim, my imagination, but plain for all to see. I have lived with your moods. I am not inventing them. I have seen you behaving like a child, crying in front of the children. So my direct experience matches what I can only suppose to be the situation in London.

163

I consider you have subjected my children to gross neglect. If you had been more involved with your parental responsibilities, rather than putting your own feckless desires first, you would never have ended up in hospital. I cannot see that you can now be considered a fit person to bring up children on the brink of adolescence. Therefore, I have decided, along with Alison, that, I will, next week, come and get the children, and that from now on they will live down here in Bristol with us, where I can start to pick up the pieces and put some order into the mess you have made of their lives. I have told your parents of my intentions and they have voiced no objection. My impression is that they are secretly relieved. They have obviously been extremely worried about their grandchildren. My mind is made up. I want no further correspondence on this matter. If you have practical affairs to arrange, you can do so via your solicitor. From now on I shall return all your letters unopened...

Subjected my children to gross mental and physical neglect...
Maybe Tom is right. Maybe love is not enough. Perhaps I should never have removed them from what they knew, to a school where the children come from three continents. What am I doing anyway looking for some spurious notion of the past, taking photographs in this alien place? Maybe it is not only the Christmas roses that failed to thrive, but my children.

She comes from Southwark. Is just filling in. They are short staffed in the Hackney office. She carries a leatherette shoulder bag and a black attaché case and wears matching court shoes with little leather bows the same shade of beige as her neatly bobbed hair and a polyester jacket with brass buttons. I have scrubbed and tidied the house. Shouted at the kids to sort out their rooms and pick up the clutter of tapes, pants and trainers from the floor. But she has already been to see Tom and Alison in Bristol. I imagine all three of them propped on the leather sofa in the book-lined study with its dark 60s William Morris wall paper, a Bach fugue just switched off as she enters the room. The studious quiet, tea on a tray. The conservatory filled with cacti and tomatoes. Concerned, responsible conversation. "Our only interest, of course, is the children. You do understand, this is not a decision we have taken lightly. But I'm very lucky to have Alison. She's more than happy to take them on. Of course she has her own academic research, but between the two of us…"

I clear a space between the boxes of photographic paper and sheets of Annie's music and hand her a mug of tea, which she leaves sitting on the table to grow cold.

"It's two children, is that right. A boy and a girl?" she says looking at her notes. "And they both have their own rooms? Good," she says, nodding, writing everything down on an official form. The skin of her hands is red, liverish against the white moons of her nails. She must have bad circulation. On her little finger is a small gold signet ring. I notice she isn't married. I try to imagine those chapped hands wiping shit from a baby's bottom, caressing a lover. But they are report-writing hands. "I'd like to be able to speak to both the children in private if I may? But first, perhaps you could show me round the flat."

"You understand," she continues, back in the kitchen, sitting forward in her chair, her legs neatly crossed at the ankles, a tanned court shoe hooked behind a beige calf, "that your recent *illness*," she expels the word on a heavy sigh "will have to be taken into consideration. There is no question of either the courts or for that matter your husband, I'm sorry your ex-husband, punishing you in any way. It is simply what is, at this point in their life, in the best interests of the children. After all Josh is growing up. Boys need a father. A role model. Perhaps if you had a partner. But it's not easy for a woman alone to bring up growing boys. You do understand," she says again, aligning the edges of her report sheets in precise

165

right angles as if in emphasis, "that I simply make a recommend-ation to the court. I decide nothing. It is up to the judge. I can see that you obviously love your children. But after your recent difficult time, well perhaps you need a break, a rest."

That night my sleep is punctured by bad dreams. It is always the same one. I wake in a sweat. I know I have been calling the child-ren. I was lost in an endless green corridor. A maze of speckled lino passageways smelling of industrial polish. I followed the signs, but all the doors were shut. It is 3.00am. I go into the kitchen. It's freezing and the only sound is the hum of the fridge. I open the door. It is empty apart from some pickled gherkins lurking in a jar on the back shelf. Tom's letter is still on the table propped between the candlesticks. I light a cigarette and breathe the smoke so deeply I start to cough. I am freezing even though I'm wearing Liam's old sweater. So it has come to this. *I cannot see that you can now be considered a fit person to bring up children on the brink of adolescence...* Outside in the small dark yard, beyond the creosote fence, comes the bloodcurdling sound of two cats fighting. My solicitor phoned me this morning to say that he has received a date for the court hearing and is concerned that Tom is going to use my stay in hospital against me. "He's an intelligent man, Hannah. He knows what he is doing. I'm worried that even if you do win today that he will challenge the decision. That it'll all drag on for months. That won't do either you or the children any good and in the end it could still all go against you. Of course, normally with a boy your son's age he would be asked where he wanted to live, but in view of the arrest and your breakdown – I'm sorry to bring that up but if I don't the other side will – I think the judge may come to different conclusions." I haven't the strength to go on, to fight any more. I have to let go. Tom, the cottage, Liam. Now Josh and Annie. And inside I feel something shatter and I know it is finally finished.

They don't say much when I tell them that Tom has decided that they will be better off living with him. Josh simply becomes more sullen, slamming doors, refusing to tell me where he is going. Annie is silent and withdrawn as we spend the week routinely washing and ironing her clothes, collecting up her recorder music and gym kit.

Saturday morning they arrive in the Volvo. Alison won't come in. She sits waiting in the front seat behind the screen of *The Times*. Tom balding and ill at ease in his studied weekend casuals, the open necked button shirt, the M&S cashmere that presumably are Alison's doing, stands awkwardly on the door step. It is as if his attire is a rebuke to my faded denim shirt and chemical spattered jeans. And suddenly I see him, as he stands there waiting for the children to bring down their bags, at twenty, with his untidy hair, lying on the floor in his college room, talking about capitalism and listening to Bob Dylan, wearing the baggy sweater his mother had knitted him. Now his voice is flat and tight. He doesn't look at me and never addresses me directly, as he gives the children a series of breezy instructions. "Your bike Josh. Are you bringing your bike? That's right Annie. Is that the only bag? Josh, really, there's not room. We'll get the speakers next time. OK? Great. Good lad. Got everything? Say goodbye to your mother now."

Belongings packed in the boot. On the pavement by the open car door, Annie's newly washed hair is silky against my lips. Josh is more awkward, shrugging me off as I try to hug him, wanting the whole episode to be over, to ensure that there is no scene, no embarrassing emotions . "Bye Mum. See yer."

Then the doors slam and the car pulls off down the street. I can see Alison fold up her paper and turn to talk to them in the back seat...

In the empty hall I can still smell them. I pick up the post. A gas bill and a surprising note from Jackie with a cheque for £50. *Thought this might cheer you up when the children go. Our love, Steve, Jackie and the girls.* I stand staring at it, not knowing how to react, what she is trying to say. I don't know whether to feel grateful or patronised. Then I go into Josh's room. It is the usual tip, although I'd told him to sort it out before he left. The walls are covered with posters of Arsenal players and rock bands. I don't know their names. The floor is a litter of dirty trainers, sweaty socks and mugs of old coffee growing mould. I pick up a pair of dirty jeans from the floor and fish for the other sock. Above the tape deck and speakers on his book case everything is tidy. His books are in neat ordered rows. *Longmans' Guide to Third Year Physics* and *À Vous La France! The Scarlet Pimpernel* and *Swallows and Amazons*. And I remember how the winter before we left the cottage, we had sat by the Aga drinking tea as it rained outside and Roger had tacked his way in wide zigzags across the steep field that sloped from the lake to Holly Howe farm, pretending to be a dinghy. *Better drowned than duffers if not duffers won't drown.* The telegram from his father had read. "What's that mean Mum? What's a duffer?" And on his unmade bed, his duvet clasped in my arms, I bury my face in his stale adolescent smell and weep.

✳

My pen scratches at the soggy pages of my note book. A chrome sky. The morning is damp and thick like wet washing that won't dry. I am walking along the edge of the Regent's Canal in the direction of Old Ford looking for ideas for new pictures. This is the arse-hole of the city, the soft underbelly. Those that were once contained and sheltered behind the high walls of asylums and poor-houses gather here like diesel sump at the bottom of an engine. This is the club-house of the dispossessed. Care in the community. The regulars each have their own spot. The bench opposite the gas-works, the steps by the rubbish bin. A couple of cans of Tenants is the accepted brew. On the far bank a man is fishing. He is sitting on a small stool, beside a can of bait, a lunch box and thermos and a large green umbrella in case it rains. The water is the colour of dull pewter but its surface is covered in a greasy film. It's hard to believe he will catch anything. As I stop to watch him I see coming towards me, out of the corner of my eye, a man with razor-cropped hair and a spider-web tattoo decorating his left cheek. On the end of a leash he has a white pit-bull. It is pulling so hard against the metal chain that the muscles in its neck bulge and it looks as if it might choke. Its fleshy pink muzzle is covered with dripping white slobber. The owner looks as unpredictable as his dog but they ignore me and walk straight past.

Now the rhythm of caring that defined my life has been broken. The domesticity dictated by Josh and Annie's needs. The ironed school shirts, the packed lunches and clean socks. I am cut loose on the daily tide. I am opening outwards like one of those gelatinous sea anemones whose hair-like filaments grasp whatever comes within its reach. I hook myself to what I see in the world around me, and as I go out with my camera, realise that real looking involves the dissolution of fear, that it is a merger, an act of sorts, of love.

Developing the negative

Della is sitting waiting on my front door step when I get back from the book shop. It's my last week. Now I only have myself to worry about I've decided to chance it and give up my two days a week to concentrate on the exhibition. She is sitting next to a vast nylon zipper crammed with shampoos, mousses, shower gels and body lotions. There is also a small portable TV and a set of heated hair tongs.

"Took you at your word, Hannah. Fucking bastard chucked me into the street," she says nodding at the surrounding clutter, her voice brittle with that over-gloss I'm beginning to recognise. "Said he'd fucking break my arse if I called the police. Found him in bed with that cunt Tanya Martin. Had to wait thirteen years to get him into her knickers. And she's got two kids. Paying me back. That's what he's doing. This fellow, he kept ringing the club, asking what time I got off work. Dave wouldn't believe me when I said I'd never laid a finger on his arm, let alone his flaming dick. Fucking hell. When would I have time? I'm either bloody working or he's the one bonking me like some demented tom cat on speed. Mind if I come in? I'm knackered," she asks her bravura slipping.

"Bought you this," she says waving a bottle of whisky. "Oh, God I've just remembered you don't drink it. OK if I use in here?" she asks marching into Josh's room and dumping the TV and nylon bag on the bed and throwing open the wardrobe. My heart jumps at the sight of his old blazer hanging limply on the back of the door, its empty sleeves vulnerable as the long white wrists of adolescent boys, the shape of his elbows imprinted in the shiny black cloth. Opening the cupboard dislodges a cascade of games kits and trainers and the room fills with Josh's smell. She turns to the small chest. "Perhaps I could put some of these in bin-bags," she says pulling out the drawers, removing his old sweaters and T shirts, "just for the time being. Make a bit of room."

I've barely got in the door and taken my coat off, let alone got used to the idea that Della has moved in. I'm not sure that I meant her to take me literally. I want to ask her how long she is planning to stay, what she is going to do if she can't work at the club, but decide against it and simply ask if she wants a cup of tea. "Still only got Earl Grey I'm afraid," I say realising I'm sounding irritated.

"Forget the tea Hannah. Go and have a shower. I'm taking you out thanks to a few extra bob on permanent loan from Dave. It was just sitting there in the safe. It's fiddled anyway. VAT. So come on. Get your glad rags on. When did you last have a night on the town courtesy of Customs and Excise? Serve him bleeding right. I'm pissed off with him ordering me around. Who does he fucking think he is anyway? Look at me," she says standing in front of the hall mirror with a playful pout, one hand behind her head seductively gathering up her hair, as she runs the other over her tight lycra top. "I'm young. Knockers the size of melons. I don't need that crap anymore."

"Della, I'm not sure. I'd been planning to work, to go through some contact sheets. And anyway I don't have anything to wear, I hardly go anywhere anymore. And my hair. Look at my hair. It's a mess."

172

"Here," she says ferreting through her large nylon holdall and bringing out a crumpled Armani jacket. Where's yer iron? Got some black leggings? I'll do it while you're in the shower." Through the bathroom door I can hear clapping as she irons the jacket in front of *Blind Date*. "Number three. She should go for number three," she calls across the hall. "He's got the best body. But it looks like she'll end up with number one though and he's a real jerk." I feel a frisson of excitement as I climb into the shower, like a teenager getting ready for the school dance or a Saturday night at the pictures.

✳

Soho. Dean Street. The French House. "This is a bit arty," says Della, pushing her way through to the small crowded bar and ordering two whiskeys without asking what I want. "Who are they then?" she asks nodding at the wall covered with black and white photos of Francis Bacon, Dylan Thomas, Jeffrey Bernard. 50s Soho.

The bar is packed. There are presenters from the BBC. Journalists on their third and fourth rounds. Ad men from local offices chatting up girls with bright crimson lips. I feel out of practice. I used to come here with Liam. We would meet after work when I could get away and walk through to Chinatown to go and eat. Golden glazed Peking duck hung in the restaurant windows, the smell of soy sauce and sweet and sour prawns seeped into the street. At Oriental City there was always a queue, despite the four floors lit with bright chandeliers like an old Chinese ballroom. On the walls there were lotus flowers and red dragons for good luck. We would have Dim Sum. The waiters rushing backwards and forwards, bobbing between the tables, with little rush baskets. Steamed crab with ginger and spring onions. I could never get the hang of cracking the claws, sucking the meat out in one, like Liam. I always seemed to leave the table a battlefield of broken shells. I'd practically need a shower, not just one of those little scented pancake rolls of hot flannel heated in the microwave. Then we might go to Ronnie Scott's. Liam had been going there since he first came to London. He knew all Ronnie Scott's corny jokes by heart. At three in the morning we'd have coffee and toast at Ed's Diner with the down-and-outs and the late clubbers. Then catch the night bus from Trafalgar Square or walk back to his place as the sun rolled up the river in a bronze ball from the east.

She is curious about Liam. "You really minded that didn't you Hannah? His leaving? I mean I know Dave's behaviour's rubbish and all that but I don't let it get to me. I stayed for the sex and my job and because of knowing each other so long" she says, nonchalantly drawing one of her long cigarettes out of its packet and holding it between her lips in anticipation of a light. A man in a crumpled linen suit leans across, and with one flick of his Zippo, obliges. "But in the end, well here I am, with fuck all, camping in your flat and I don't give a shit," she says with a throaty laugh, exhaling a cloud of blue smoke through her pursed and painted lips. "Plenty more fish in the sea," she winks and nods in the direction of the extinguished light. "You see, you should be more like me."

I smile. "I'm not sure I'm up to it Della. Anyway, I don't think I'm really ready for another relationship yet."

"Who said anything about a relationship? You can have a good time. You don't have to live like a flippin' nun. Now I've got this little plan. See my friend Lindsy who used to be at the club, she's just had a baby. Cute little thing. Dropped out like a flipping pea. Well, of course with a baby, the hours and that are bloody useless. So know what she does? Telephone work."

"Telephone work?"

"Yer, you know those sex lines. Some sad git phones up from a telephone box, hasn't had it off for weeks, you talk him through a blow job and Bob's your uncle – if you'll pardon the expression. No touching. No mess. Portable phone. Do it in the bath. Good money. And it leaves me some time free. What you think?" she says taking another sip of whisky.

I'm amazed at her brio. And as she expands the details of her plans, I try to reconcile the image I still have of her, bruised and vulnerable on my futon, her head tipped back to drain her glass of wine, exposing the line of thick tan make-up where it met the white skin of her throat like the edge of a mask.

"Isn't it dangerous? I mean couldn't they find out where you live or something?"

"Nah. They have to phone a number in the paper. It's routed via Hong Kong or Guyana or somewhere like that. Costs them a bloody fortune, only they don't know till they get the bill and the wife goes mental. Anyway that way I can pay my share of the rent."

I feel my resistance growing and fear for the invasion of my space. I wonder if I am ready to live with anyone else, the absence of the children is still so raw. But when I try to express my doubts she shifts on her stool, her body stiffening slightly and her eyes narrowing dark and sulky as a child's, waiting to see if I'm going to spoil her plans.

"As I said," cajoling her "of course you can stay for the minute. But if or when the kids come back we'll have to find you somewhere else."

Her mood lifts and she knocks back the rest of her whisky. "Come on. I'm bloody starving. What you fancy? Indian. Chinese? You choose. It's on me. Anyway there's no need to worry about the phone. I'll get a different number."

"Italian, I think. I love Italian food," and she hooks her arm in mine, as if she has known me for years, as we turn down into Frith Street, past the chic gays drinking cappuccinos on the corner, like a couple of school girls playing truant.

"You like dancing?" Della asks, scraping out the fluffy egg-yellow remains of a zabaglione from a tall glass in a little restaurant in Greek Street.

"You know, I can't honestly remember, Della. It's not something I've done for years."

"Well now's yer chance. Come on let's go back to the East End. Hoxton. The Bass Clef. We'll get a cab."

There is no point in protesting and anyway I'm beginning to enjoy her company. She is generous and though I insist, she won't let me pay for a thing. "Put your money away. As I said, this is courtesy of HM Customs and Excise. Anyway you're doing a favour keeping me company."

The basement is a crush of bodies. The music is African, the beat like a thick pulse in the smoke-filled dark.

"Come on let's dance," she says her jangling bangles running up and down her bare arm, her gold hoops bobbing in the stretched lobes of her ears. As we dance we are joined by two Jamaican boys. There is no conversation. We just enjoy the dance and their loose-limbed fluid movement. It is hot and airless and our clothes stick to our clammy bodies. One of the boys wears a leather waistcoat with a shirt open to the waist. His skin is glistening with sweat. The room is all sound. And as we move closer and closer in the crowd, sound, music, touch, meld as he slips his hands around my waist, his grape skin against my face, his lithe body loosely swaying, swaying next to mine.

∗

Desolate February Days. London looks so bleak. It is always best when the weather is neutral, not too hot not too wet or cold. It feels as if these cold grey days will never end. I have to push myself to work. I phone the children when I can but it's hard to speak to them and I try not to think about Liam, try to live in a continuous present.

I never hear from him. I am steeped now in these East London streets. The markets, the canal and Whitechapel have become my daily reality, I feel almost completely disconected from my past. It's like a twist of apple-rind that once peeled from the fruit simply shrivels and turns brown. Occasionally my mother phones me. Her voice is brittle. She always brings the conversation back to the one subject I try to avoid, the children. She will insist on attempting to convince me that their being with Tom is the right thing, that life must be better for them now they no longer have to live in the East End. She has always hated my coming here. My return offended her sense of natural progression. She doesn't seem to have any sense that I am bleeding invisibly under the skin like an emotional haemophiliac.

Great Orex Street. On the left, on the corner, is a boarded up building with a *For Sale* sign for an *extensive freehold site*. It is built of low red brick. Dirty net curtains hang in the metal framed windows. Above the doorway it says *The Kosher Luncheon Club Morris Kasler Hall. The last Kosher Eating House open to the public. Est. 1930s.* And immediately I am back in the London I came looking for when my father was a young boy. The London of my Grandma Millie and Grandpa Dan. A London of urban humour and respect for education, where the Beckies and the Zeldas and the Berts and the Sams met here daily for lochen soup and chopped herring, to gossip and argue, debate and cry over the fact that they had survived, had overcome the horrors of the East European pogroms, to recover a little dignity and self respect in the cobbled alleys. I can hear those intense, insistent voices, the broken guttural English, the thick Yiddish as the old complain about the young with their lack of respect for religion or interest in politics. "Ach, the youth Harry. No sense of tradition. That's how we survived." And so they had, stitching themselves to the fabric of the host culture, as young cabinet-makers, tailors and cobblers. While those hungry for ideas,

177

hungry for something more than the long hours in dank workshops, flocked to the Jubilee Street Anarchist Club to hear talks on Morris and Shaw, Beethoven's Fifth.

As I walk down the narrow street, the surface breaks for a few yards into cobbles, then as I turn the corner, they merge again with the new asphalt. The road is a palimpsest. Accretions of history are layered like strata of rock. Now it is lined with young trees. Behind the neat garden fences with their carousel washing lines and Sky TV saucers are new bungalows with mock fan-shaped Georgian doors and small gardens filled with white plastic plant pots. Those I came looking for are long gone, dead or very old. A few spinster aunts, widows and crumpled old men remain marooned by illness and history. But their children and grandchildren have all gone to become teachers and solicitors, film makers and politicians. They left by way of Hackney and Tottenham en route to Hampstead and Hendon. What was it Captain Edwards of the Salvation Army said when I went to Booth House, that the East End had always attracted those who didn't feel they belonged. And as the watery autumn sun goes in again, and it starts to drizzle, so I have to hurry towards the tube before the downpour, I understand why I came.

Normally when I get back to the flat Della is asleep or out. Sometimes I might catch her watching *Neighbours* or in the bath, her hair caught up with a tortoiseshell comb, portable phone tucked under her chin talking to a client as she lies soaking in a froth of bubbles, the bathroom misty as a tropical rain forest. I'm glad I insisted her phone had another number.

"You're fabulous, big boy. I'm wet now, really wet," she murmurs huskily, winking at me across the triangle of white tiles visible through the open bathroom door at the joke, as she snuggles beneath the foam.

This afternoon I'm tired. I'm coming to the end of traipsing the streets. I've more than enough film. Now I need to spend time in the dark room, printing, highlighting, cropping. I'm not sure that I can catch the threads, the interconnections that I've been trying to establish. I still feel like an amateur, even though since the children left I've done nothing but work. I flop down on the futon under the *Madonna of Mercy* to read my horoscope. I haven't given them up. I still dream.

It is then I notice that the Turkish cover has been crumpled and that on the far side of the futon, by the wall, there is an empty whisky bottle and a mirror covered with talcum powder. I look closer knowing that neither of them is mine. Scattered across the floor are scraps of kitchen foil. I can't believe what I'm seeing. I get up and go and shout for Della. There is no reply. I call again and knock on Josh's door but there's no answer. I assume she must be out so go back and look at the mirror again. It is covered with a film of white dust. I draw my finger through it. Smell it. I don't know what I'm looking for. But I know I'm not wrong. All the anxiety I felt with Josh comes rushing back. I don't want anything to do with any of it. I go back and open the door to Josh's room. There is Della spread-eagled in a black suspender belt next to a sleeping Dave. On the bookcases above Josh's bed, next to *Tintin* and *The Scarlet Pimpernel*, is another bottle of whisky. Dave's expensive suit lies chucked on the floor. He is snoring. On a tanned wrist, flopped across his bare chest, is a heavy gold Rolex

"For fuck's sake Della. What d'you think you are doing?"

"Oh yer. Hi Han!" she says reaching lazily across the sleeping Dave for a silk wrap on the back of the chair. As she stretches over him her left breast droops heavily against his cheek. "Didn't think you'd be back for while."

"I gather that. Would you please get him out of here. *Now.*" I scream as he stirs, then rolls over.

I can't believe it. Can't believe after what he did to her she would invite him here to my flat. My son's room. I must have been mad ever to let her move in. The blind is drawn although it's only three o'clock. The room smells of whisky and sex. On the floor a used condom damply oozes its contents onto the rug. I march back into the main room, my room, and pick up the dust-filmed mirror.

"And what the hell is this?" my voice is trembling, outraged with a sense of betrayal, as I thrust the offending object under her nose while she groggily wriggles into a pair of knickers salvaged from under the duvet.

I go into the kitchen to wait for her. I can't stop shaking and rummage through my bag for my roll-ups. As I lean against the sink, inhaling deeply, trying to get a grip, Dave pushes open the door with his foot. His hands are busy tucking in his shirt, zipping up his flies. He is tall, well built. I know he works out at the gym.

"Della tells me you got a problem, Hannah. That right? Not getting enough then? Jealous cause we got no one to get into our nice clean middle class knickers? You make me fucking sick. Think you're fucking lady bloody bountiful. Didn't realise Dell's been seeing me for weeks did yer? Can't keep away. Not with her itchy little cunt," he says slipping his arms into the silk-lined sleeves of his jacket and slamming the front door behind him.

"I would have told you, honest," Della says slinking into the kitchen like a guilty child that's been caught thieving, pulling tight the sash of her robe, holding it together at the neck, as if to regain some modesty. Her eyes are smeared with mascara. She's a mess.

"How could you? How could you sleep with a man that beats you? And here, here in Josh's room. You've had cocaine in Josh's room," I say bursting into tears.

"Hannah. You don't understand. He's my bloke, we've always been together. I'm no good without him. It was Tanya Martin that did it. Saw her down the Mile End Road the other Saturday. Bloody crowing she was. He's *my* bloke Hannah. Even if he is a right shit some of the time. Can't you understand? Thought I could do it on me own. But I'm nothing without a fella and one's much like another, so I might as well stick with him. It's all right for you. You've got your photographs. Me, my talent's sex. What'm I going to do on my own? Look I'll go and pack me things."

I'm too upset to say anything to stop her as she goes into Josh's room and starts to decant her belongings from the drawers, carelessly stuffing lacy bras and screwed balls of stockings into her large nylon bag. The bathroom begins to seem very bare as she collects up her pots of hair gel and mousse, the *Ambre Solaire* self-tan, and curling tongs. When she's ready she slips on her black leather jacket, then tilts her head first left, then right and slips her gold hoops into the holes in her ears, then runs her fingers through her blond hair. Neither of us seems to know what to say.

"Right then, better be off," she says breezily, then softening "Hannah. I know you feel I've let you down. You've been a good mate, we've had a few laughs. No hard feelings?" she says extending a manicured hand. "I'll only be two floors down, I'm moving back with Dave, so'll probably see you around. Though now I'm going back to work at the club I expect we'll keep different hours. Still hope the show goes well. I'll go and see it when it's on. Funny I've lived here all them years and I've never been inside that place," she says picking up her nylon zipper and stuffed carrier bags. "See you later then."

I watch with mixed emotions as she totters downstairs, curling tongs, hair dryer and all her bottles poking from her bag then shuts the door. The flat seems very silent and I realise I'll miss her. Perhaps Dave is right. Perhaps I am jealous. Jealous that for her sex is fair exchange, easy currency, has been from the days at the back of the school lavatories when Tanya Martin dared her to touch Steve Fisher's thing. When she realised it wasn't such a big deal and that he was so grateful. They all were. Just for a look, a quick feel. And I wonder if I could have been more like that with Liam. Uncomplicated, satisfied only with pleasure, relinquishing the desire for osmosis.

The room is getting dark. As I go to the window and watch the children coming down the street from school kicking up the leaves in the gutters they come back unbidden, insistent, those afternoons when I was working at the bookshop and Liam collected Annie from school and I would come home and find them bent over her homework at the kitchen table with a mug of tea and hot toast. And suddenly I am overwhelmed with longing. For his tongue in my mouth, his rough stubble against my face and wonder if I will ever be able to make all this – work, taking pictures – seem like enough.

This is my London. It has nothing to do with Liam. Unlike all those places I cannot go because he has a claim on them, has marked them with his presence. Columbia Road, Greenwich, Camden Lock. Places that I need to restore to my map of the accessible city, where I still expect to see him in every shop or café. It is strange how those we have loved and lost leap out at us from every street corner, haunt our waking even when we try to forget. For when I go to Camden it is still always Christmas. We are there looking through the market stalls for a present for Annie, the air thick with the smell of incense and baked potatoes. Stall holders stamp their icy feet in heavy moon-boots. He found her tiny silver earrings shaped like unicorns. Magic earrings. "Are these *just* from you Liam?" Annie had asked quietly, "Not *you* and Mummy? Are they just your special present to *me*?"

And still I cannot walk through Chinatown. It was there, on the corner, that he poked the corner of his handkerchief under my eyelid to get out a speck of grit. These are the things that make up love. The banal transmuted into memory.

Now the camera gives me a single focus. I don't have to consider

what goes on outside the frame, that small square in the view finder.
I decide to take the tube to Tower Hill, then catch the Docklands
Light Railway. I have been so concerned with history perhaps I
should go and look at the future. A tourist in my own city, I wait
beside the Meccano railtrack with a group of Germans in expensive
casuals, and Japanese students with backpacks and cameras. They
all have guide books. What do they expect to find in the Isle of
Dogs? What do the gleaming office towers, the new designer flats
with their river balconies, entry phones and security systems signify
for them? This is Lego Land. The train, all shiny glass and blue and
red chrome, curls along its Toy Town track, past the small balconies
of endless grimy council flats festooned with lines of washing, and
the wide new picture windows of arrogant office blocks. Both the
poor and the wealthy, it seems, are doing battle for the same shared
fields of blue sky.

On the opposite bank of seats sit two, presumably retired,
couples. The women wear pearls and Jaeger prints, their grey hair is
neatly blown-dry. Their husbands wear brush cotton checked shirts
and brown suede brogues. I feel uncomfortable being part of this
invasion of anthropologists witnessing the disruption of a
community. This new colonisation. A group of French school
children all rush to the right of the carriage as the train halts on a
curved hump of track beside Canary Wharf glimmering magnificent
and hubristic in the autumn sun, towering like an ancient citadel
over the mariner. The glass is smoky and impenetrable, a *No Entry*
sign reflecting the nosy outer world back peremptorily on itself.

From Island Gardens you can descend by lift to walk under the
river via the Greenwich Foot Tunnel to the south bank. I can see the
tall masts of the *Cutty Sark* marooned in its dry dock. The magnificent white stone facade of Wren's Royal Naval College, elegant and
urbane beside the squat cubist factory chimneys, the dark grid of
empty gasometers and blue chemical cylinders. The tide is out.

Small waves lap the little beach of sandy mudflats. They are strewn with flotsam and jetsam. Old tyres, a broken bucket, plastic bottles and driftwood. There is the smell of salt on the breeze. A single skuller rows past on the wide shimmering water against the backdrop of gantries and dredgers. *Wimpey* cranes dip their giraffe necks into the black water below Lovell's wharf.

It is a glorious day. By the river wall a middle aged man with an easel is painting the view in water colours. He nods good morning, asks if he has taken my place. "Best spot here." I stop and chat. He is friendly and asks about the camera, what I do. He gives me a local history lesson. "The Naval College was built by Wren. Was a hospital before it became the Royal Naval College. Don't actually come from round here myself but it's certainly changed. The trouble is these new houses," he nods to the spruce waterfront maisonettes "haven't gone to the locals. They brought in a lot of coloureds." I decide, before he says any more, it's time to move on.

I pass an old stone wall and between two buildings notice a slipway leading down to the water. A small notice says that this is the landing place of the old Greenwich Ferry, Potter's Ferry, that was run by Greenwich watermen from the 14th century. And suddenly I am there standing on the same mud bank where Pepys climbed ashore. And I think of all those hundreds and thousands of invisible lives that have peopled London through the centuries, lives that for a moment flickered like the moths before the storm lantern on summer evenings in Somerset and then were gone. Civil servants, market traders, shop keepers, rat catchers, refugees who made up the warp and weft of the hidden city, all now disappeared, lost like bleached negatives leaving no trace or stain of the small intricacies of their unrecorded lives.

It is midday and the low autumn sun burnishes the corrugated river pewter and chrome as it winds its weary way towards the silted reaches of the Thames Estuary and the Isle of Sheppey. A plastic bottle and a McDonald's carton float past. And suddenly I realise that this is it: this mellow morning, here and now, watching the oil-streaked water, breathing in its damp pungency as a white swan drifts by, its wings puffed into white sails like those of an Elizabethan barge carrying its regal charge from Hampton Court to Greenwich. *Sweet Thames, run softly...* and suddenly I understand that I am neither the sum of my past nor defined by my possible future. That this brief moment, here on this muddy bank, with the steel cranes in the distance glinting and dipping their heads like giant birds, is itself a kind of love. Across the river a pleasure boat is turning in an arc across the wide reach, taking its passengers back up past St Katherine's Dock and Canary Wharf towards Tower Bridge, back in a circle to where earlier in the day they had embarked, their journey now ended.

As I walk towards the Island Gardens' station, I pass an elderly man on a bench looking out over the river. He is spruce in a neat V neck and pressed grey trousers. Beside him is a holdall out of which he fishes his plastic box of sandwiches and a thermos and a notebook bound by an elastic band. Perhaps he comes here every day. I try to imagine a life made up of such inconsequential meagre events. I get off the train at Canary Wharf and treat myself to a glass of wine by the river, watching secretaries in short skirts chattering over cocktails, flirting with young men with mobile phones from Accounts. When I change back onto the Circle line, I feel as though I have been away for months in another city.

✳

It is weeks since I've seen daylight. The show is only six weeks away and I've been living like a troglodyte in the dark room. I have to have all the work finished within the next ten days so it can go to

185

the framers. I've been experimenting with different textures of photographic paper, scratching the negatives so they will pick up flaws and imperfections like a lived in body. I worry that I haven't been true enough to my subjects. Multiple meanings reveal themselves not foreseen at the moment when the shutter closes. It is a form of alchemy. Ugliness and poverty become transformed by isolation and framing into a certain stark beauty. Mary, the old testament head of Winston, the portrait of Captain Edwards, each has its own pathos. Frozen moments. Time already lived and spent, dropped like the petals of a blown rose. Vulnerable lives moving towards their own dissolution; all attest to time's relentless melt.

I'm pleased with some of the still-life and urban landscapes. Princelet Street Heritage Centre with its empty arc, the jam jars of dead flowers, cobwebs, the box of old candle stubs. The fretworked balcony taken in the evening half-light resonates with the ghostly presence of lost women as the men busy themselves with the affairs of the service below. These are revelations of the city's many un-named truths, its hidden corners, its gross extremes. What my camera seeks out is the jetsam, the dross; recycling everything the careless city discards. I print up the hoarding advertising for machinists and Hoffman pressers on the gate of the old factory in the Mile End Road, on different grains of paper. Each one was taken at a different point in the day as the light changed. Will they tell anything of those hidden lives, the lost stories of those who came from Lithuania, from Derry, from the Indian sub-continent. Fathers, grandfathers, brothers, children, wives, with their battered cases and brown paper parcels, to struggle among the heavy steam irons, the smell of damp cloth in airless work-rooms, to set down roots and reinvent themselves so as to merge quietly into the drab surroundings in this alien land.

Lead transmutes to gold in the mosaic of aubergines and marrows stacked on a market stall, in an old woman's toothless smile.

186

The final print

It's foggy as I make my way to the gallery. A velvety November fog, the sort seen most often now in 50s films where the heroes are bent beneath felt homburgs, the collars of their macs turned up against the damp. It's rush hour and Whitechapel is chockablock with traffic, the headlamps damp stains of chrome yellow on the tarmac. Vegetables, broken cardboard boxes lie sodden in the gutters. I got a card this morning, shoved through my letter-box, from Della. A kitten holding a silver horse-shoe for Good Luck. It was kind of her. I've not seen her since she left, our hours are so different. I wonder if Dave is treating her any better. I'm glad she got in touch. Marion offered to come to the gallery with me but I said I'd meet her there. I need some time alone to collect myself. It's not just anxiety about the opening and the weird mix of people who will be there. My parents. Jackie. Josh and Annie, whom I've hardly been able to see over the last few months, and other photo-graphers come to check out my work, maybe a critic or two if I am lucky, it's that I still feel thrown by the letter – reading something so long after it was written, so long after the event – and I'm really upset about Mary. It was mere chance I found out. This morning I was in the library with some flyers for the exhibition – I'm quite convinced there aren't any in the whole of London – and bumped into Captain Edwards from Booth House who stopped to thank me for my invitation. He was touched, he said. Hadn't expected it. I have noticed Mary hasn't been around for some weeks. She usually hangs round the steps of Christ Church, her and a few others with nowhere to go. She likes the company. I ask, if by any chance, he has seen her. He knows all the homeless, the down-and-outs. Tries to keep tabs on them. It must have been the change in the weather. Some school kids found her early one morning in the doorway of an Indian take-away. Bolt upright, still holding her bags. Stiff with cold and death. I can't get the picture of her out of my head: of her wheezing in the damp night air, coughing up green goblets of phlegm from her useless chest. The slow black slide into unconsciousness. Dying alone, defiant, sitting up. Face to the fucking world. She's been buried already. There was no one to mourn. It was a pure formality, a pauper's funeral. I wonder if any of her children will ever know, ever care. What was the point of all that unredeemed hardship, all that pain? Yet in her own way, she never gave in. What would she have made of the huge black and white photograph on the end gallery wall, blown up larger than life-size like some 18th century society portrait by Joshua Reynolds, skirts coquettishly pulled up around her bloated knees, that mock Marilyn Munroe pose and seductive carious smile. Fame, she'd have called it with her self-deprecating sense of mockery. I wish she was here to see it. I really miss her. I can imagine her in her three smelly coats with a couple of Safeway carrier bags standing in the middle of the polished gallery floor, oblivious to the embarrassed half-glances, face to face with her own image. "Sure pet, you could have made me a little lovelier."

I feel the weight of Liam's letter like a stone in my pocket as I walk from the tube. I've been carrying it around for weeks, it's almost falling apart, though I have stopped reading it so often now. This morning I knew I was trying Marion's patience. She had warned me not to send him an invitation, pointed out that the letter had said all there was to say. But I sent one anyway. "He could have at least answered, Marion. Not to reply. Forgodsake not to say anything. Not even Good Luck. Nothing." I had exploded, stomping round the kitchen, unable to let go, to let the matter drop, as I banged piles of washing up into the sink. On the crowded pavement the tide is running against me. People scuttle wrapped in scarves and heavy overcoats against the unfamiliar fog in a stream towards the bright mouth of the underground. Lights from the cut-price leather shops and take-aways smudge the wet pavements. Buses throw up fans of muddied spray. It has suddenly turned cold. I'm expected at the gallery early but can't face it yet and turn into Brick Lane and go into The Three Stars pub. I've never been in here before. A woman with hennaed hair and orange-peel thighs is half-heartedly gyrating her hips just out of time to the music. She must be at least 40. She wears a black nylon G-string and suspenders. Her breasts are flaccid as if lacking conviction in their own eroticism. There's a ladder in her stockings and her white stilettos are scuffed at the heel. It is still early and the few men in the pub stare into their pints ignoring her, unimpressed with what she has to offer. She glances disinterestedly in my direction. Desire, or even its semblance, doesn't seem to have any part here. This is simply what she is paid to do. And the men caught in their own sodden half-thoughts ignore her, just as they ignore the racing on the TV in the corner. I leave and go across the road to the pub in Heneage Street. By contrast it's crowded. Artists, office workers, local East Enders. Noise amid the traditional red plush and mahogany. In the corner by the electric log fire I make a roll up, taking time to get the edges of the paper just level. Then pull the letter out of my jacket and re-read it for the hundredth time but it offers up nothing beyond the

189